WELL OF SOULS

SECRETS & SIN: BOOK 2

LINSEY HALL

© 2022 BONNIE DOON PRESS, INC.

1

Cora

I was in over my head.

Like, _way_ over my head.

The thought was a litany repeating itself as I stared at the chaos around me. I was _so_ not qualified to run the bookshop that I'd inherited from a miserable mother I'd never met. Books were stacked on every surface, haphazard piles that threatened to fall over and crush any passing mice—of which there were _plenty_.

The only way I was going to finish cleaning up this shop before I died was if I turned into Cinderella and got the little interlopers to help me out.

Unfortunately—or fortunately, maybe—my demon

cat scared them away. It was about the only thing he did, besides sleeping on top of the toaster.

"You know, I don't think it's that bad," Fiona said.

The ghost sat on the edge of the jumbled desk, swinging her transparent legs back and forth. Wild curls scattered around her head, she grinned at me.

I gestured to the heaps of books. Many of the volumes contained scintillating subjects, like tax law or coin sorting. "What about this motley collection is *not that bad?*"

She shrugged. "So your mother had bad taste in books. You'll make it work."

"Not bad taste. *That* I could work with. Bad taste is subjective. But I think it's fairly objective that the majority of my potential customers aren't in the market for *101 Farming Laws From the 1890s* or *Valuable Coins from the 1920s.*"

She grimaced. "Fair point. So what will you do?"

"Clear most of this out. Make the good stuff look nice, I guess." There were a few hundred fiction titles and spell books I thought people might be interested in, though I wasn't really qualified to say. My only experience with books was reading them, not selling them.

And the last week of sorting and planning had proved one thing: you can take the girl out of the mercenary squad, but you can't take the mercenary out of the girl. I was hopeless at this.

A loud yawn sounded, and I looked over to see Balthazar, my demon cat, waking up from his umpteenth nap on top of the toaster. It was his favorite place to sleep, and his red eyes blazed with contentment, his shadowy midnight fur wafting in the non-existent breeze.

"It was nice of you to bring his toaster down here," I said to Fiona.

She laughed. "Oh, I didn't do that."

"What?" A chill ran down my spine. "Was someone else here?"

"No." She shook her head. "Balthazar dragged it down by the cord a few days ago. He likes the company and wanted to hang out with us."

I stared at the grumpy bastard, impressed. "Well done, Balthazar."

He stared at me blandly, then pressed the button on the toaster with his paw, turning it on, and went back to sleep.

Right.

I returned to the books and began unpacking a box I'd found in a dusty corner. In the week I'd spent cleaning the shop, I'd had dinner twice with my friends, Mia and Rei.

The person I *hadn't* seen was Talan, the demon lord of New Orleans.

"Have you seen Talan, lately?" Fiona asked.

I glared at her. "Can you read my mind?"

She shook her head. "No. But you've got that scowl

on your face, and I'm working on a theory that it has to do with him."

"Well, you're not wrong." I raised my brows at her. "And you also know I haven't seen him, because you go everywhere with me."

She shrugged. "True. But he could always appear in your dreams."

"Well, he hasn't." That was one of his particular powers, and he'd used it only twice with me—neither time recently. "Which is good."

"You sure?"

"Yes!" We'd shared a kiss that was hot as hell, and he'd done a few really nice things for me—like kill the man who knew my secrets and threatened my safety—but he clearly didn't want anything to do with me.

I wanted to keep it that way, especially since I was pretty embarrassed by the fact that I'd waited four full days for him to come see me before I'd given up.

Silly.

It wasn't like I could trust him. I couldn't trust anyone, especially not the demon lord. He made my blood heat, and that kind of loss of control was unacceptable. I couldn't afford it.

Anyway, I had my friends, the only people in the world that I was actually beginning to *maybe* trust. It felt as unnatural as riding a giant tortoise in the Kentucky Derby, but it was happening.

I grinned at Fiona, the best of the lot. When I'd

moved to New Orleans a couple weeks ago, she'd welcomed me by throwing books at my head. I never would have guessed we'd become friends, or that I might have something like a home here.

A tiny buzz of warmth filled me at the idea. I'd always wanted a real home. Being raised in an orphanage and sold to a mercenary guild would do that to a person.

But I'd never truly believed I'd get one. Even now, as I cleaned up the apartment and bookshop that my mother had given me, I didn't really believe I could make this into my home. The idea was just too foreign. Too impossible.

Still, I wanted it. Silly as it was.

Things had been going so well this last week that it was making me almost jumpy. Life didn't work like this. Not for me, at least.

As I stared at the box of books in front of me, I realized they were different than the others I'd found. For one, they looked old. And valuable. Magic vibrated from them, more intense than any I'd ever felt coming from a book.

"Hey, come look at this," I said.

Fiona hopped off the desk and knelt beside me to inspect the books. "Huh. Those look valuable. And kinda familiar, in a weird way."

"You've seen these before?"

"No, and I'm not sure why they look familiar. But

they do."

I carefully closed the box. "I'll have to find someone to ask about them. Do you know anyone?"

"Maybe?" She frowned. "The weird thing about being a ghost is that you forget some things about your life. And your death."

"Your death?"

"Yeah, you know I don't remember the details. Most ghosts don't. I just wish I knew."

I patted her awkwardly on the shoulder, my hand disappearing an inch into her transparent form. "I'll help you figure it out, I swear."

"I know. Thanks." She looked to the side. "So, uh, I have something I maybe need to mention."

"Ugh. Bad news?"

She nodded.

"Good," I said. "Things have been going too well lately. Makes me nervous."

"Well, you're not going to like this." She glanced toward the shop window, worry flashing across her face. "I think someone has been watching the shop."

"Watching?" A shiver of ice ran through my veins. "Like, a stakeout?"

She nodded again. "I've only seen the guy twice now, but he's been standing in the same place, hidden by the shadows."

"Damn it." I dragged a weary hand through my hair. "And you're sure he's watching the shop?"

"Yeah, he just stands there, watching. Couldn't see him well because of the shadows, but he was definitely there."

"When?"

"Last night and this morning."

"So, not long then."

"Of course not." She glared at me. "I knew you'd want to know."

"And you don't think it's one of the demon lord's goons?"

"They wouldn't hide. And I'm not sure he's keeping tabs on you like that."

Heat flushed my cheeks, the sting of embarrassment making me look away. Of course he wasn't. He was done with me now.

I shook my head, driving away thoughts of him. "Probably my old boss." I hated the idea that he'd already found me. "I didn't tell him I was leaving."

"Your boss can't stalk you all the way here."

"Oh, he definitely can." And he hadn't been just a boss. Technically, he'd been my master. He'd bought me from the orphanage and forced me to join his kill squad, so he believed he owned me.

I'd kill him if he came anywhere near me ever again.

"Well, we've got your back," Fiona said.

Warmth flushed through me like the rays of a winter sun driving away the chill. "Thanks."

"Anytime." She rose to her feet. "Now, I've got to get to—"

Her form flickered in and out of existence, anxiety crossing her face. Her gaze moved to mine, eyes wide. "I don't know what's happening."

I jumped to my feet and ran toward her, my heart racing as she disappeared for a second, then reappeared.

"I'm being pulled away!" Her voice was squeaky with panic as she reached for me.

I grabbed her, trying to wrap my arms around her transparent body. I could touch her, but it was a strange sensation, like holding onto Jell-o. I gripped her as hard as I could. "Hold on, Fiona!"

"They're too strong!"

I couldn't see who she was talking about, but I could feel them pulling at her. Fear tightened my grip as I fought to keep her from being dragged away. "Hang on, Fiona!"

Talan

I stepped through the portal, letting the ether drag my exhausted body. When the portal spat me out in the basement of my house in New Orleans, relief rushed through me.

I was only minutes away from a shower. After trekking across the burning wasteland of my underworld, I was in desperate need of one. That, and a cold beer. Preferably at the same time.

As I strode toward the stairs that led to the main part of the house, I felt the power pulsing from the portal. It felt a bit strange, but at least it wasn't weak. That soothed me. I might not have gotten the answers I sought about my mate, but at least the spell that kept my demons on Earth—something that shouldn't be possible, but I had made it so—was still going strong.

Still, I wished I'd gotten answers about Cora. How was she my mate if she wasn't a demon? It was rare, but not impossible for a demon to have a non-demon mate. But I didn't even know what species she was. There had to be more to her, things I didn't know about.

At the top of the stairs, I nearly ran into Liora.

My second-in-command stumbled back, her dark eyes wide. The close-fitting leather clothing she wore had been designed for fighting, and the sword at her side was her best friend as far as I could tell. She inclined her head, dark hair falling in front of her face. "Apologies, my lord."

"Talan is fine." I frowned at her. She only used *my lord* when something was wrong. "What happened?"

"Disappearances." Worry tugged at her face. "Three demons from our part of town. They all disappeared at exactly the same time."

"What do you mean, 'disappeared?' Kidnapped? Left town?"

"No, like poofed out of existence. Here one moment, gone the next." Her eyes darkened with worry.

"There are witnesses?

She nodded. "To each situation, yes."

I dragged a weary hand through my hair. "This isn't good."

"Do you think they've gone back to our underworld?" she asked.

"Not willingly." Everyone was here in my part of New Orleans because they wanted to be. Earth was a hell of a lot nicer than the underworld we'd come from. It had taken a lot of magic to create the portal—also known as the Well of Souls—that kept us here on Earth. It was the only one of its kind, and I'd created it.

Which meant it was also my job to keep everyone safe, since I'd brought them here.

Guilt streaked through me. I'd been off searching for answers about my mate while my people had been in danger.

I needed to keep my head in the game, or I risked losing everything I'd built. More importantly, I risked failing those who relied on me.

"Do we have any clues?" I asked.

"Not yet." She reached into her pocket and pulled out a small card. "But I do have more news. Weird news."

"Weird?" I frowned as I took the small card and flipped open the heavy cardstock. It was an invitation—from the *fae*. I looked up at Liora. "What the hell?"

She nodded, eyes wide. "Crazy, right?"

"Very." The fae hadn't invited me to their annual bacchanal in ten years—not since I'd refused the first invitation due to a prior commitment. It was one of the biggest events in the city, and definitely the biggest event hosted by the fae. Their queen had been so offended by my refusal of the prior invitation that she hadn't issued another.

It was fine with me. The fae were a tricky, unreliable group who lived out in the bayou. Since they didn't have territory in the city itself, they weren't on the Council with the other factions—the demons, witches, shifters, and vampires.

I turned the card over, as if the back would reveal its secrets. "Any idea why they're inviting us?"

She shook her head. "Not a clue. Unless it's related to the disappearances."

Anger—hot and cold at the same time—rushed through me. It was possible. I had no idea why the fae queen would take some of my people, but she had the magic for it. And it was good leverage.

But what did she want?

"We'll go," I said. "In the meantime, get the elite guard to find out anything they can about the missing demons."

"Will do."

"Thank you." I turned and headed down the hall. Now that I had a party to attend, I really needed that shower. The beer had become a pipe dream, though.

Whatever the fae queen wanted from me, it would be dangerous.

2

Cora

I barely managed to pull Fiona back from whatever was trying to drag her away. It had been a tug of war with an invisible force, but I'd won.

For now.

Fiona panted and slumped against the desk, her face stark with fear, dark eyes wide. "What the hell was that?"

"I don't know." I tried to keep my own fear out of my voice, but it was slithering through my veins. Cold sweat had broken out on my skin, and it felt gross.

I had no idea what had threatened Fiona, but I couldn't bear to lose her. "Do you think it will happen again?"

She shrugged, worry flashing on her face. "I have no idea."

I chewed on my lip. "We need to figure out what's going on."

"How?"

"A seer?" They sometimes had answers. "Maybe Mad Maury knows."

"The guy in the graveyard?" She shivered. "I'm not a big fan of that place."

"I know, but it might be your only hope."

"Yeah, but—"

A knock sounded at the door, cutting her off. I looked between Fiona and the sign in the window, which had been flipped to open. "Why is someone knocking? We're open."

She drifted to the window and peered out. Her eyes widened. "It's a fae."

I felt my brows pop up. "Really?"

She nodded. "Which explains the knocking. They don't come to town often, and it's not their way to just walk in."

"Huh." I hadn't seen many fae in my life. They often lived in their own communities, many of which were on a separate plane from the Earth that the rest of us lived on. "Well, there's only one way to find out why they're here."

I strode to the door and opened it, ready to call on my Karambit if I needed it. The fae were fast fighters, but with my little blade, I was nearly unde-featable.

The man on the step was tall and slender, with long golden hair and the ethereally beautiful features common to the fae. His pale silver tunic and trousers were embroidered by an expert hand, and the bow that hung over his back was a thing of beauty.

He inclined his head, the golden hair falling away to reveal his pointed ears. He handed me a small square of fine parchment.

"What is this?" I asked, taking it carefully to avoid touching hm.

"An invitation."

Fiona gasped behind me.

"We hope to see you there." He gave a small bow, then disappeared.

"No way." Fiona drifted up to join me, leaning over my hand to look at the invitation. "I can't believe it."

"What do you mean?" I opened the card to see *The Bacchanal* written in scrolling script, along with a time and place. "It's just a party."

"Just a party." She laughed like a lunatic. "Just a party. You're hilarious!"

"So it's more than just a party?"

"Duh." She grabbed the invitation and held it up to the light, as if to check that it was real. "It's *the* party of the year, and the invitations are worth a mint."

"So why were we invited?"

She shrugged. "Because you're new in town? I don't know. But I do know that we're going."

"Is it safe?"

She shrugged again. "Don't know. I've never been. But I want to go."

"We've got a lot on our plate. We need to figure out why my mother killed you and how you almost disappeared a few minutes ago. That was kind of a big deal."

She grimaced. "No kidding. That was scary. Got any ideas? Because I don't."

"No. So, we definitely don't have time for a party."

"But we do." Cunning glinted in her eyes, and it reminded me that there was a core of steel beneath Fiona's party girl exterior. "The fae have one of the most powerful seers in the city. Better than Mad Maury. If we go, we can try to talk to them. See if they know anything about what's happening to me."

I frowned. That was a good reason to go to the party. Still... "Feels like too much of a coincidence for you to need this type of help right before an invitation shows up."

"Maybe, but do we have another option?" She nudged my shoulder with her own. "Anyway, I've got you with me. We'll be fine."

Maybe. Maybe not.

But I didn't like this coincidence.

That didn't mean I wasn't going to the party. I'd go

and figure out what the hell was going on, but I'd be careful and bring help.

"You know what this means, right?" Fiona asked.

I shook my head. "No, what?"

"Makeover!"

"Ah, of course." I didn't own anything suitable for a party, but our friend Mia did. "Maybe we can bring her as backup. And Rei."

"No harm in trying." Fiona grinned. "It'll be a girls' night!"

I'd have preferred wine and movies—much less opportunity for the fae to double-cross us in that scenario—but I liked her idea. We'd stand a much better chance of getting what we wanted and avoid trouble if we had our friends with us.

"All right. Let's go talk to Mia."

Mia was in her coffee shop. She called in her support staff and helped me pick out a sleek black jumpsuit. The silky fabric felt like heaven on my skin and looked badass.

She chose a cobalt dress to match her hair, and Rei went with red. The red should have clashed with the witch's pink hair, but somehow it looked great on her tall form. Fiona, unfortunately, was a ghost and couldn't change clothes, watching wistfully as we got dressed.

"You, okay?" I asked.

"Yeah!" She waved her hand dismissively, but the cheer in her voice was forced. "I was never much into clothes anyway."

Mia gave her a deadpan look. "Really?"

"Fine, this sucks." She heaved a sigh. "But at least I'm a ghost and not totally dead, right?"

Worry tugged at me, the memory of her disappearing making me fidget. What if she started to permanently fade? If it happened again, I might not be able to keep her on this plane. And if she left, where would she go?

"Hey, Earth to Cora." Fiona waved her transparent hand in front of my face. "Come back from wherever you've gone."

I blinked. My worries had sucked me in. How long had I been out? "Sorry, just thinking. Is everyone ready?"

Mia and Rei nodded, and Fiona shrugged and said, "Always ready."

"Then let's go."

We trailed out of Mia's house, Fiona and Rei chatting about the party. As we climbed down the stairs to the cafe on the bottom level, Mia typed into her phone, calling us a car. New Orleans had a magical version of Uber, apparently, and the purple hearse that pulled up made me raise my brows.

"Really?" I asked.

A green skinned man got out and grinned at us, revealing a double row of fangs. Despite the chilling points on his fifty-odd teeth, there was a friendly cast to his eyes that made me like him immediately.

"Ladies! Looking good." He pulled open the back door of the hearse. "We headed to the party of the year?"

"Yep." Mia gave him a grin and climbed into the back.

"All right, well, I'm Walter, and I'll be your chauffeur tonight. Help yourself to the waters in the back. Hydrating is important!"

As I stepped toward the car, I thought I caught sight of a shadow of a person standing across the road. I squinted into the dark, trying to make out the details, but the figure melted into the shadows.

I blinked.

Had I even seen anything at all?

"What's wrong?" Mia asked.

"I thought I saw someone across the street. Did you see anything?"

She shook her head. "No, sorry."

"It's cool." I pushed the thought away and followed Mia into the car. It had been done up a little like a limo, except the strange proportions of the space made it impossible to forget the original purpose of the vehicle.

I caught sight of Fiona's grimace as she climbed in and tried to squeeze her hand. It didn't work great—

hard to make contact with a ghost, but she shot me a grateful smile.

When pop music pumped out of the speakers and colorful lights started flashing overhead, her smile turned more genuine.

Walter peered through the tiny window that separated our part of the hearse from his. "Let me know if you want different music."

"This is good," Mia said, moving to the beat.

"Then enjoy the ride. We'll be there in thirty minutes."

"Excellent." Mia reached into her large bag and pulled out a bottle of champagne.

I raised my brows. "When did you stash that in there?"

"I can't give away all my secrets." She grinned and popped the top off, then took a sip straight from the bottle and passed it around.

When it reached me, I tilted the icy, sweating bottle up to my lips and let the fizzing liquid spill over my tongue. It felt divine, and with the music thumping in the background, it felt like I was in a music video.

Despite myself, I *did* enjoy the ride. I hadn't expected to, but I'd never done anything like this before.

As we pulled up to the fae estate that was located deep in the bayou, Walter lowered the music. I peered out the curtained windows at the tangle of wild forest that bordered the road. Massive trees hulked in the gloom, their branches draped in shroud-like Spanish moss. Tiny white lights sparkled between the trees, drifting like snowflakes of pure magic.

Faerie lights. I'd heard of them before, but never seen them. They were supposed to be an offshoot of the magic that kept the fae realm tethered to Earth, and I swore I could feel the sparkle of their power against my skin.

"Almost there, ladies," Walter said. "Brace yourselves."

As the car slowed, the magic swelled, pressing in on me almost unbearably. Rei and Mia grimaced, though Fiona didn't seem to feel it.

"We're passing through the portal that leads to their realm," Rei said. "The gate has been made visible for the party, so that everyone knows where to go."

I spotted a large silver gate as we drove through, shuddering as magic swelled in the air.

I was *not* a fan. When the car finally popped out on the other side and the horrible pressure abated, I slumped. Like many fae realms, their territory was on Earth, but not quite. If one didn't go through the portal, a person could walk through their land without ever seeing them or their buildings.

Fortunately, we'd been invited to go through the portal.

As the car joined a line of other vehicles creeping slowly toward the party, the view outside the window became more fantastic with every foot we traveled. Flowers with massive blooms clung to the tree branches, hanging from emerald green vines. The blooms glowed, brilliant clusters of pink, red, and orange, more beautiful even than the flowers in the demon lord's garden.

The sound of music trilled through the forest, filling the interior of the car with a strange melody that relaxed me even further.

"Careful," Mia said. "Don't fall under their sway too much."

I shook myself. Shit, she was right. I'd become distracted by the pleasures around me, and I was still inside the car. We weren't actually here to have fun, no matter how cool the place was.

I turned to Fiona. "So, where do we find this seer?"

"I'm not sure, but I'll figure it out."

Okay, not what I'd been hoping for, but I had to have faith in her.

Walter pulled the car to a stop and leapt out, opening our door before we could get to the handle. I climbed out, immediately hit by the magnificence of it all. The magic that perfumed the air smelled sweetly of flowers, with an earthy undertone of the bayou.

Music filtered through the trees, something played on string and wind instruments that threatened to carry me away in a trance. I shook my head, trying to break it.

Despite the beauty of our surroundings, the danger

in the air was thick and potent, and I looked at my friends to see if they sensed it.

As if she could read my mind, Mia said, "It's part of the allure. The best part of the year, but with a hint of danger."

"A hint? I'd say it's more than that. But where does it come from?"

She shrugged. "Being in the bayou so close to the gators? From the fae themselves? We're in a place that's normally forbidden, so that could be it. I'm not sure. But nothing bad has ever happened at one of these parties, so I think we'll be fine."

"There's a first time for everything."

She wrapped an arm around my shoulder and laughed, then turned me to look at the crowd.

There were dozens of fae; their ethereal beauty and pointed ears made them unmistakable. But there were vampires and shifters and witches, as well. People milled around tables piled high with delicious food and drank from crystal goblets that sparkled under the moonlight.

Acrobats flew through the air at the edge of the clearing, leaping off tree branches and doing maneuvers that made my stomach plunge just from watching. I turned to my friends, noticing that Fiona was already gone.

I hoped that she was off looking for the seer.

"Let's go check out the buffet." Mia grabbed my hand and Rei's and pulled us forward.

Leaves crunched underfoot as we walked toward the massive table set with towering trays of pastries. A rainbow of frosting decorated the tiny cakes with swirls and dots in ornate designs. Sugared flowers adorned each miniature confection, making them look like tiny gardens.

Next to the cakes was a tiered, mouthwatering display of cheese. Every variety in the world had to be present, along with bread that smelled fresh from the bakery, its soft interior surrounded by a crunchy exterior.

I looked farther down the table, spotting displays of meat, fruits, and chocolate—all arranged so beautifully that it looked like artwork.

"We can eat this stuff and not be trapped, right?" I asked, remembering the old fae legend that was still true in some courts.

"Definitely," Mia said. "They don't want us stuck here anymore than we want to be."

Excellent. I reached for a tiny pink cake and ate it in one bite, my eyes nearly rolling back in my head at the divine taste of butter and sugar.

"A beverage, ladies?" The smooth voice drew my attention, and I turned to see a handsome fae man with rich auburn hair and eyes the color of fresh grass. He held a tray of crystal goblets, each filled to the brim with sparkling golden liquid. A single flower bloomed in the middle of each glass, so beautiful that it made my heart ache to look at it.

This place was *insane.*

I'd never seen such magnificent things, and I *definitely* wasn't the type to be moved by the sight of a flower suspended in champagne.

"Absolutely." Rei took two and handed them to us, then grabbed one for herself and grinned at the man. "Don't go far, now."

He smiled and bowed before turning away.

She looked at us, her gaze turning serious. "Just a few sips, especially since we drank that champagne in the car. We need to be on our game for Fiona."

She was right. No matter how delicious the drink —and it *was* delicious, the way it popped with freshness on my tongue—we needed to keep our wits about us.

That didn't mean we couldn't eat our fill and pretend to be having the time of our lives. The fae didn't need to suspect we were here to mooch off their seer, and it wouldn't be hard to pretend to enjoy myself at a party like this.

We watched the crowd as we grazed. The canapés were amazing, and if I'd brought a purse, I'd stuff a dozen of them inside for later at home. Surely, Balthazar would enjoy a treat from here.

Unfortunately, my only option would be to stuff a

meat pastry into my cleavage for him, and I was fairly certain that was a bad plan.

All around, the party flowed. People laughed and talked and ate, danced in front of the acrobats, and lounged on cushions surrounded by flowers.

But there was something in the air that I hadn't noticed when I'd first arrived. Tension and danger, an invisible haze that tightened around me, warning me. This was not a safe place.

I caught Mia watching me. She leaned forward and whispered, "You feel it, don't you?"

I nodded. "What is it?"

"The fae are dangerous. Incredibly so. They've weakened the magic here to help facilitate the party, but their realm isn't always pleasant for outsiders. We're not used to it."

"And people still want to come to the party?" I shivered.

She shrugged, grinning. "The danger adds excitement."

"You have a point, there." I'd had enough excitement from danger in my life, but even I felt more alive while standing amid it.

I turned back to the buffet. I'd just shoved another tiny cake into my mouth when my gaze snagged on the demon lord.

3

Cora

I stared at Talan, riveted by the sight of him. He stood on the other side of the clearing, as devastatingly handsome as ever. He towered over most of the other guests, his broad shoulders and warrior's stance standing out even amongst the fae, who were no slouches in the super-hot warrior department.

His dark clothing was expertly cut, casual, and yet fantastic. But it was impossible to look closely at what he wore when his face held my attention. Sharp cheekbones, full lips, and eyes that burned straight to my soul.

I swallowed the cake just before his gaze snagged with mine, and I felt the heat of it down to my toes. It felt like we were connected by an electrical current that stretched across the ether. It lit me up like a firework. Every atom in my body exploded with awareness, and I was suddenly a fawn trembling in front of a predator.

His gaze swept over me, something possessive blazing in his eyes. At his side, his hand clenched into a fist.

Why?

Was he angry with me?

Or did he want to reach for me, yet forced himself not to?

Ha. As if.

And I hated how weak he made me. How distracted. When he was nearby, he became the sun that my attention orbited around, and it was unacceptable.

When he turned and walked away, I was equal parts relieved and disappointed.

Silly, stupid girl.

My friends were watching me with wide eyes. Rei's cheeks bulged like a hamster's, a half-eaten cake dangling on her lips as she studied me.

"You should swallow," I said.

She chewed and gulped. "Yeah. Just...that was quite a show."

"What do you mean?"

"I mean that I almost saw fireworks light up over your head when you saw him."

"Same for him," Mia said. "He looked like he wanted to eat you alive. In the good way."

The idea made heat flush my cheeks, and I turned away, looking for Fiona. "We came here to find the seer, and we need to get to it."

I didn't see Fiona, but I did spot another woman in a gown so sparkly that it looked like it was made of diamonds. She carried herself with the grace of a queen, an effect heightened by the crown on her golden head.

Rei whistled low from beside me. "Her royal highness has made her appearance."

"Queen of the fae?" I asked, even as I knew the answer.

The woman looked around at the crowd with an expression that screamed *I own you*. Definitely the queen.

When her gaze snagged mine, I stiffened. Her brows raised, and intrigue lit her eyes, then she looked away.

"Well, that was weird," Mia said. "She made eye contact with you, and she doesn't do that with anyone."

Mia was right. Though the queen was looking at everyone in the crowd, she wasn't really looking *at* them in the same way she'd looked at me.

A shiver of unease ran over me, but I filed the mystery away for another time. I needed to focus on Fiona right now.

As if she'd heard me thinking about her, Fiona appeared between the trees in the distance, her glowing form a beacon in the dark. She waved us over, her face excited.

"I think she's found the seer." I started toward Fiona.

Rei and Mia followed, but not before each had grabbed two more treats to eat on the way. I did my best to shove Talan from my thoughts as I slipped through the crowd. There was enough space in the forest that it wasn't packed body-to-body, but it was still a tight fit.

By the time I reached Fiona, my head was back in the game. All I had to do was think about the horrible feeling of her body being pulled from my grasp, and it brought me back to the present.

"Well?" I asked, stopping in front of her. "Did you find the seer?"

She nodded. "Yep. Pretty sure I did. Come on."

We followed her through the forest, moving away from the crowd. The sound of music drifted after us, punctuated by laughter and excited yells. But as we got deeper into the bayou, the sounds of hooting owls and screeching animals replaced the music. To my left, a large, low body rustled in the underbrush.

When a head featuring bulbous eyes and a hundred fangs revealed itself from beneath the foliage, I lunged backward.

The gator just stared at me indifferently, and I hurried on.

Finally, we reached a clearing where the faerie lights were thicker. Thousands of them swirled through the air like a light show made just for us. I stopped and stared, awed.

"This is it," Fiona said.

"Really?" I looked around for a person and saw no one.

My friends joined me, and we stood side by side amongst the lights.

"Seer of the Enchanted Forest, are you here?" Fiona asked, her voice imploring.

Lightning struck, piercing the ground next to us in a brilliant bolt of light. I jumped, stomach in my throat. Thunder boomed, so loud that my head rang.

"Holy fates, is that her?" I asked.

Fiona winced. "Maybe? She might be in a bad mood."

Lightning struck again, bright and bold, blinding me. My heart thundered against my ribs as I whirled around, looking for the seer. Suddenly, all the danger in the air made sense.

This place was deadly.

"Please, we need your help," Fiona shouted. "You may take some of our energy, willingly offered."

I looked at Fiona. "Wait, what now?"

"It's our offering to the seer," she said. "We need something to entice her to help us. And to make her corporeal."

Of course. Nothing in the world was free.

Lightning struck again, the charge of electricity in the air making the hair on my arms stand on end.

"We might need to get out of here," Mia said. "This isn't going well."

"One more try," Fiona said. "It's the night of the bacchanal," she coaxed the seer. "You could use the energy we give you to attend."

The air shivered with magic that didn't feel quite so deadly, and I straightened, looking around. A presence had arrived. More importantly, the lightning had stopped.

Sparkling faerie lights swirled around us, faster and faster, rushing through our bodies and making me shiver. Weakness pulled at me as the lights took some of my energy, and I stiffened my spine.

Finally, the wild ride was over, and the lights coalesced into a figure, a golden beacon glowing with an inner light. Her simple dress concealed a tall, slender form.

She stretched her arms as she yawned, her pretty face contorting. When she smiled, it was so brilliant that she could have fueled a nuclear bomb. "The bacchanal, you say?"

Fiona nodded. "Yep. It's just begun, too."

"Oh, excellent." She grinned with pure pleasure. "They always forget about me on this night."

How could anyone forget about her? She was so glorious and powerful.

Or maybe they were just afraid of her. It was probably intentional that the seer wasn't invited.

"We were hoping you could help us with something first," Fiona said.

The woman nodded. "Of course. A few answers about your future, I presume." She looked straight at me. "Your fear is correct—your past is hunting you. And it *will* catch you."

Cold raced through my veins. "Really? When? How?"

She nodded. "Be wary. Also, be wary of the demon lord. He will try to claim you, but the road is paved with danger."

"Uh—" I stared at her, stunned. This wasn't what I had expected, and as much as I wanted answers, I couldn't get greedy with her time. "We're here to talk about Fiona." I inclined my head toward my ghostly friend, still stunned but trying to pull it together. "She almost disappeared earlier today."

Fiona stepped closer to the seer, fear shivering through her voice. "It felt like a dozen hands were trying to pull me away from this plane."

The seer frowned, her gaze searching Fiona's face. "Yes, I see that. It is a curse—one that is affecting more people than just you." She paused, closing her eyes as if to search for information. When she opened them, they blazed with warning. "You don't have long left."

"What is it?" I demanded. "How do we stop it?"

"Your first answer can be found in underground New Orleans."

"There is no underground in New Orleans," Mia said. "The water table prohibits it."

"That's not entirely true," I said, cold rushing through me. "There is one place."

And it was at the demon lord's estate.

Talan

I walked through the crowd, almost blinded by the memory of Cora.

I hadn't seen her in a week, and when my gaze had landed on her across the clearing, it had felt like crashing into the sun. Heat had rushed through me, followed by the most intense desire to stalk over and pull her into my arms.

This desire felt like it was almost entirely out of my control, and I couldn't abide that, not when I needed to spend all my energy protecting my people.

I had to stay away from her.

Through the trees, I spotted Liora. My second was dressed in her usual attire—nothing would get her in a dress—and she walked through the crowd with her keen gaze trained on her surroundings. She wasn't here for the party any more than I was

We were here to figure out what the hell the fae queen wanted from me.

When the queen's second-in-command approached me, I wasn't surprised. He was nearly as tall as I was, with the easy confidence of someone who knew how to use the blade at his side. I couldn't trust him, but at least I could understand him. We were similar types, two men fully committed to protecting our people.

"Her Highness would like a word with you, Demon Lord." His tone suggested it wasn't a request, but that didn't bother me. I wasn't used to being commanded, but if I didn't want to follow orders, nothing on heaven or earth could force me to do so.

However, I'd come here to satisfy my curiosity about the invitation, and he was offering me those answers. "Lead the way."

He nodded and turned, gliding through the crowd as if he walked on clouds.

I followed him, declining a passing server's offer of wine. Roughly one hundred yards later, we reached a clearing in the woods filled with dancing people, a band set up on one side. Across the clearing, a raised dais was topped with the most ornate throne I'd ever seen. A woman sat upon it, glaring out at the world like she owned it.

And she did—at least this little part of it. Just as I owned the demon sector of New Orleans. I stopped in front of her, raising an eyebrow. "Well?"

She smiled, a cunning curve of her lips. "Demon Lord. I'm so glad you could make it."

"I'm keen to find out why you called me away from the city."

She nodded and stood, gliding down the stairs that led from her throne to the leaf-strewn ground. As she passed me, she said, "I thought we could have a drink over here."

"Lead the way."

The dancers parted to let her pass, the fae bowing as she walked by. Some of the other guests bowed as well, but they were awkward compared to the lithe grace of the fae.

The fae came into the city so rarely that I'd hardly ever seen the queen. I certainly didn't come here. I had no reason to.

But the downside was that I didn't know much about her, other than the fact that she was rumored to be power hungry. That, I could understand. But I would need to take every opportunity to learn what I could while I was here, and her people's behavior was a clue to her personality.

She took a seat at a silk-clad table that had been set up at the edge of the dance floor. Two ornate chairs were positioned next to each other, tilted so that they had a view of the action. Fairy lights sparkled overhead. The damned things were distracting, and I looked forward to being back in my own territory.

She sank gracefully into one of the chairs and gestured for me to take the other. I sat, and two uniformed men swept forward and held out trays of beverages.

I took one but didn't drink, asking instead, "Why am I here?"

She sipped her sparkling champagne, smiling over the rim. "A little romance."

I felt my brows rise. Technically, she was attractive. All of the fae were. But I felt nothing. Obviously, she felt nothing for me—there wasn't the faintest spark—but the fae were a bit old-fashioned in some ways. Marrying for power wasn't unheard of. I had the best territory in New Orleans, and she had none in the city. Perhaps she wanted access to that?

She laughed. "I can see the wheels turning in your head. And no, I didn't bring you here for me."

"Then what?"

"For her." She smiled and pointed across the clearing. "Your mate."

The words sent a shiver down my spine, and I turned to look. Immediately, my gaze snagged with Cora's. It was the second time I'd seen her tonight, and it hit me just as hard as the first. My chest clenched, and my breath ran short as I took her in.

Beneath the fairy lights, her dark hair gleamed, and her skin was pale as ivory. The black silk of her clothing draped over her curves in a way that made my fists clench, an unconscious gesture that I had to force away.

"Pay attention to me, now." The queen's voice broke my concentration, and the feel of her hand on my shoulder made me twitch uncomfortably.

I turned to her, and she drew her hand away.

When I spoke, my voice was harsh. "How the hell did you find out about her?"

She smiled and shrugged. "I have my ways."

The seer. It had to be. The fae were famous for having a powerful seer living in their woods. She must have heard about Cora from her.

But what was her angle?

"I brought her here for you." The queen's brows rose. "Aren't you pleased?"

"I could see her any time I want. There is no need."

"But you *haven't* seen her. A whole week has gone by since you've seen her last, so I thought I'd push fate along a bit."

Unease crept over me. "Why are you spying on me?"

"Oh, you're not special." She laughed. "I spy on everyone."

It should have made me feel better, but it didn't. I'd missed the spy she'd set on me because I'd been too distracted by Cora.

Another reason she was bad for me.

"Is that all?" I asked, hearing the annoyance in my voice.

"Well, I suppose." She frowned. "I thought you'd be pleased."

"No, you didn't." She wasn't stupid. She'd know that I wouldn't want her meddling. And yet, she still had. There was more she wanted, but I wasn't going to find out tonight. "I'll be going."

"But—"

I strode away from her, heading toward the exit.

4

Cora

As soon as my gaze met Talan's, I turned away, heart racing.

He was sitting with the fae queen, and yet his eyes burned into me like a hot knife through butter.

"What's he doing with her?" Mia asked.

"No idea." I didn't look back, even though I wanted to. "Haven't seen him all week."

"They're both basically royalty," Rei said. "Maybe they get together all the time."

The idea made a faint surge of jealousy shoot through me, but I forced it away. There was no reason to feel jealous. He was nothing to me.

"Let's get out of here," I said. "We got the information we came for. If he's occupied with the queen, then maybe we can sneak into his house and check out the basement."

"You really think it's in his basement?" Fiona asked, frowning.

I shrugged. "Do you know of any other underground spaces in New Orleans?"

"No." She sighed heavily. "You're right. We need to check it out."

"I'll call the car," Rei said, pulling out her phone and dialing. When she was done, she looked up. "Should be here in about ten minutes. I'm going to hit up the buffet one more time."

"Oh, me too!" Mia said.

Seeing Talan and the queen together had stolen my appetite, so I just waved them on. "I'll go wait for the car."

"I'm going with them, if that's okay," Fiona said. "Haven't seen action like this in forever."

"Sure. I'll see you in ten."

They hurried off, and I went toward the exit. I was nearly there when a uniformed fae stopped me, a polite smile on his face. He bowed and handed me a piece of paper. "From the queen."

"What?" I frowned as I took it, confusion flickering through me.

He disappeared before I could ask any questions,

and I opened the paper as I walked slowly toward the exit. The words on the page stunned me into stopping.

You are the demon lord's fated mate.

I blinked down at the message, dumbfounded. His fated mate?

I'd heard of them, but there was no way this was true. I turned to look for the queen, but I couldn't spot her through the crowd. What was she playing at? This was crazy.

And why was she interested in me?

I was a nobody, new to town.

Carefully, I refolded the note and stuck it in my pocket. I couldn't disregard it, but I didn't want to think too much about it. Fixing Fiona's problem was the most important thing right now, not whatever weird mind games the fae queen was playing.

It was dead quiet as I arrived at the drop-off area, the bustle of cars arriving having fallen off as the night progressed. But the party was in full swing, so no one was leaving yet. I felt a bit bad dragging my friends away, but Fiona's life—such as it was—depended on us figuring out what was going on in underground New Orleans.

That had to take priority.

I waited in the sticky heat, tapping my foot as I counted the minutes until the car would arrive. Thoughts of Talan and the fae queen circled in my mind, but I couldn't come up with anything that made sense.

All around me, the bayou was alive with life. Wind rustled the trees, carrying with it the sounds of animals and insects that were almost desperately loud, as if they competed to be heard over each other.

Despite the distraction of my surroundings, I felt his arrival before I saw him. It was like the air had changed, coming alive with an electric current.

Unable to help myself, I turned.

He stood ten feet away, stopped dead still as if he'd seen me and lost the ability to walk.

Ha, as if.

You are the demon lord's fated mate.

The words on the queen's note echoed in my mind. With Talan right in front of me, it was impossible to put them aside. I strode up to him, heart racing.

Of course he smelled amazing. Like fire and spice, so *him*. The scent of it wrapped around me, drawing me closer. He was so tall that when I stood right in front of him, I had to crane my neck to meet his gaze.

The blue fire in his eyes blazed as he looked down at me. The electrical tension that had filled the air between us was as strong as ever. It sparked against my skin and seemed to push me toward him.

The words burst past my lips before I could stop them. "Am I your mate?"

When I heard them, I almost winced. I hadn't meant to do that, but I couldn't seem to help myself.

He drew in the faintest breath, a sign of surprise that I hadn't expected to see. And yet, there was no denial.

The truth was in his eyes.

"I am, aren't I?" I said.

He shook his head, but when he spoke, there was no strength in his voice. "No."

"Why would you lie about that?" Helpless fury rose inside me.

"I didn't."

"Omission is a lie." I glared at him. "You knew about this all along, didn't you?"

His jaw tightened. "It's more complicated than that."

"Oh, really? Because from where I'm standing, it doesn't seem that complicated." And it pissed me the hell off.

I was in control of my life for the first time ever. I'd spent every other year under the thumb of someone else —either the orphanage or my old master. I wasn't going to lose that by succumbing to the whims of fate.

And fate was powerful here. Supposedly, it was impossible to fight the true mate bond.

Well, not for me.

I would not be falling for this or him.

He glared down at me, clearly debating what to

say. But there was nothing to talk about. We were done. We'd never even started, so that would make it easy.

"Just stay away from me, okay?" I spun on my heel and stalked back toward where the car would pick us up.

With every step I took, I felt his gaze burn into my back. I couldn't help the heat that rose in me in response. There was just something about him that swept me into his orbit—but I was done being anyone else's accessory.

Fortunately, the purple hearse pulled up as I reached the road. I had the back door open and was already inside by the time the driver had gotten out, and I must have been giving off some pretty intense vibes, because he just nodded at me and said nothing.

I caught sight of Talan through the open door, still staring after me, his eyes blazing with something I didn't recognize. My friends appeared. Hurrying to the car, they gave him a wide berth, and I turned, staring straight ahead.

They piled in, their eyes on me.

"What was that about?" Mia asked. "I could feel the tension between you two like the air was on fire."

"I'm his mate," I blurted, still stunned.

"Wait, what." Rei stared at me, her jaw slack.

"Yeah. Apparently, some demons have fated mates, and I'm his. Except he lied about it."

"Is it really such a bad thing to be his mate?" Fiona asked.

"Are you serious? Yes," I said. "I don't want to be bound to anyone. *I* want to make the choices about my own life." I could feel my heart pounding in my chest. It beat so hard that it almost hurt, and I pressed a hand to it.

"Hey, it's okay." Mia rubbed my arm. "Want to talk about it?"

I looked up at her, surprised. "Talk about what? We are talking about it."

"You're clearly having a panic attack," she said. "You've turned stark white, you're breathing like a line-backer trying to line dance, and I can hear your heart-beat from here. Clearly, there's something else going on."

I drew in a shuddery breath. She was good at reading people. And part of me wanted to confide about my past life since it was clearly still haunting me. They were my friends after all. But the idea of sharing something so personal with anyone... Showing weakness like that?

I couldn't do it. I knew a normal person could. Someone who didn't have my trust issues or shitty past.

But I wasn't normal.

And I couldn't share.

I'd never told them about my past, and I wasn't going to start now.

"I'm fine." I smiled and drew in a steadying breath, then looked out the window at the bayou. The wild trees whooshed by as the car made its way back to the city, and I tried to drive Talan from my thoughts.

Talan

She knew.

I dragged a weary hand over my face and sighed, leaning back against the seat of the car as it drove back toward the city.

That encounter hadn't gone well. I probably should have told her sooner, but that hadn't seemed to be the heart of the issue. She hadn't liked my omission, but what she'd really hated was the knowledge that she was my mate.

I could see it all over her. The life-altering kiss that we'd shared more than a week ago had clearly been a one-off for her. She wanted nothing to do with me.

And it was for the best.

I didn't have room in my life for a mate, especially when I'd spent the last decade thinking I'd already lost one. That pain was more than I wanted to go through again, and I couldn't afford the distraction.

Finally, the car pulled through the gates of my estate

and rumbled slowly up the drive to the house. The wild garden spread out on either side of the vehicle, and I looked out the windows, drawing calm from the sight.

This garden, and the part of New Orleans that I'd carved out for my demons, was as unlike my underworld as anything could be. Full of color and life, it was everything I'd worked for.

I needed to focus on that—especially since three of my own had gone missing. Just last week, there'd been one kidnapping. Now we were up to three.

Something was seriously wrong, and it was my job to find out what it was.

The car stopped in front of the house, and I climbed out into the warm night air. Crickets screeched into the dark, accompanied by the low croak of the bullfrogs that lived in the creek that wound through my property. The cacophony was as familiar and welcome as the sight of the garden.

I climbed the stairs to the front door and entered the main foyer. The staff was abed, and I appreciated the solitude. I didn't have the patience for niceties at that moment.

But as I walked toward my suite of rooms, I felt something strange in the air. I stopped in the middle of the hall, letting the sensation run over my skin.

Power pulsed from down below, a strange sensation that I'd never felt before.

The portal.

Shit.

Worry chilled my skin as I strode to the stairs that led to the magically created basement. I took the stairs two at a time, my concern deepening as the feeling of *wrong* increased.

When I reached the portal, I stopped several feet away. The silver light pulsed with power, white wisps of smoke wafting out of it. The portal appeared to be flickering in and out of existence—here one moment and gone the next.

That had never happened before.

The Well of Souls—as the portal was known—was usually stable. It was home to immense magical power, a stable link to the underworld that allowed me and my demons to stay on Earth. It was *everything* to us, and something was wrong.

My heartbeat thundered and my skin chilled.

I had no idea what was going wrong. Though the portal had been created using a little bit of every soul that lived in my city, most people didn't know much about it. That secret was mine to keep, and as long as my demons got to enjoy life here on Earth, they didn't mind giving the tiniest piece of their soul to ensure it.

So who had come here to toy with it? And what was their goal?

Rathbine.

It had to be. My old master had wanted my territory from the beginning. A couple weeks ago, we'd realized that someone was making inquiries into how I'd created my part of New Orleans. Liora and I had paid Rathbine a visit, and we'd left convinced that it was him.

We'd threatened him. I'd wanted to kill him, but I hadn't. To do so would violate the rules of the demon Council, which was made up of representatives from the most powerful demon species. Rathbine was on the Council. So was I. But to kill another was a statement of war against the entire Council. They would come after my people if I murdered the bastard, and I couldn't risk that.

But now that he was meddling even more...

I needed proof to bring before the Council. It was the only way to walk the delicate line between diplomacy and death that would keep my people safe.

There was no time to waste. I walked through the portal and let it suck me in and spin me through space. It spat me out in the Outer Bounds, the territory at the edge of my former master's land. The dark wasteland spread around me, the scent of blood and smoke thick on the air. Metallic clouds roiled overhead, mirroring the turbulent silver river that cut through the black and red ground.

I ignored the sight and strode up to the two guard towers that punctuated the massive wall surrounding the bastard's castle.

I felt nothing as I looked at the walls that were built of blood-red stone and jet-black mortar. Jagged parapets and soaring towers made it look like a cross between an ancient fort and a horrific prison.

For me, it had been a prison.

I turned my attention to the towers and the demon guards who stood atop them. Their horns were tipped in silver, and their crimson coats matched the pennants that flickered in the foul wind.

I stepped into the light so that they could see me, and they immediately rushed to open the gate.

It might not be my castle, but no one here would dare get on my bad side by denying me entry.

I strode through the gate, passing the skeletal trees that were hung with the bodies of executed prisoners. They swayed in the breeze, a gruesome reminder that some demons never changed.

As expected, Megreth met me at the door of the castle. Rathbine's housekeeper had always been alert to visitors, and she looked at me with wide eyes as I approached the door.

"What brings you back so soon?" she asked.

"Where is he?" I demanded.

"In his suite," she said, stepping back to allow me to enter the castle.

"Take me there."

She hurried around me and led the way down the hall. Though I was now fully in control of my fate and my life, I still didn't like being here. The reminder of my time in captivity was enough to chill my blood, and I looked forward to getting my answers and getting the hell out.

The hallways were built of black stone dotted with torches every fifteen feet or so. They gave off a faint glow as their rancid smoke rose toward the ceiling. Megreth stopped in front of a large wooden door, twisting her hands in front of her. "He won't like to be disturbed."

"Then it's best you leave. I won't tell him you brought me here." I had no love for the housekeeper, but I also didn't care to get her in trouble.

She hurried off, and I didn't bother knocking as I pushed open the door and entered an opulent living room.

Red velvet and gold filled the space, a garish setting for such an ugly demon. Rathbine looked up from an ornately carved wooden table where he sat with three other demons. His small eyes glinted with annoyance— until he spotted me.

Then the expression changed to fear.

Good.

I would use that fear, and any violence I needed to, in order to get the answers I wanted.

I recognized the other demons who sat with him, poker cards spread out in front of them—Belial, Moloch, and Valberith.

Council members.

Of course.

The slimy bastard had backup. He was too cowardly to do something like this on his own.

Belial, Moloch, and Valberith looked up at me, confusion on their faces. Rathbine's expression of fear changed to one of cunning, and he smiled.

"Talan. What a dreadful surprise. Here to join us for a game?"

Obviously not, but my plan to threaten him wasn't an option now. I didn't want the other Council members to see that—especially not before I found out if they were involved, too.

It would be far more difficult to take them all down, and I'd need to use stealth and cunning rather than brute force.

"Here to take your money," I said, pulling out the fifth chair and sitting. "How long have you been playing?"

"Oh, hours, now," Belial said. Her flame red hair surrounded jet black horns that were slender and curved. She licked her lips, looking me up and down.

I ignored the lascivious expression.

"Hours?" I took the cards they handed me. "All of you?"

"What are you getting at?" Rathbine asked, his eyes glinting.

The bastard knew something was up, of course. The damage done to the Well of Souls had happened while

I'd been at the party—I'd have felt it if it had been done sooner.

I shrugged. "Just curious how much money you've lost."

He growled, but the other demons laughed.

"I've spent the last three hours cleaning him out," Valberith said. He was a slight demon, his form wispy and insubstantial. It didn't mean he was harmless, though. Far from it. The slightest touch from his nearly incorporeal fingers, and one would face their greatest nightmares.

Moloch smiled. "From the time we start playing, no one is allowed the leave the table."

I raised a brow. "Really?"

"Cheaters." Moloch grinned. "Don't want someone sneaking off to the bathroom to stick a card up their sleeve."

I wasn't liking the sound of this. Either Rathbine had a genuine alibi, or all of these demons were in it together, covering for one another. Either way, I was going to need to be cleverer about getting my information. At the very least, I'd have to threaten Rathbine another time, when there were no witnesses.

"In that case, I'd probably better not stay." I laid my cards down and stood. "Not sure I have the stamina to stick around that long."

It was a bold-faced lie, and they surely recognized it,

but I didn't care. I wanted to keep them on their toes, so if they thought I was up to something, it was good.

"I'll see you later, Rathbine." I made sure the threat was evident in my voice. As much as I knew I should keep my enmity a secret, I wanted to scare him.

From the fear in his eyes, it was evident that I had.

5

Talan

I arrived back home with little more information than I'd gone with, unfortunately. At least the portal was stable once more. It pulsed with the same unpleasant magic as usual but wasn't flickering in and out of existence like it had been earlier.

I gave it one last look and made my way up the stairs to the main floor. I was nearly to my quarters when Liora ran up, her face flushed. She was accompanied by a young woman who wept copious tears.

"What is it?" I asked.

"As soon as I got back from the fae party, I got news of more disappearances. Three demons. One minute they were here, the next, they were gone." She looked at the woman beside her. "This is Meralie. Her husband disappeared.

My heart thundered. "When?"

"Less than an hour ago," Meralie managed through her tears. "I have no idea how it happened, though."

"An hour ago?" My mind raced. "The Well of Souls was flickering in and out of existence then."

Liora's face went white. "What? That's never happened before."

"Not that we've seen," I said. "But I felt it as soon as I got home and went to investigate. Something's wrong with it."

"And this was happening at the same time as the disappearances." She frowned. "Could they be related?"

"I don't know, but I think so."

"Was the portal flickering when the other disappearances happened?"

"I'm not sure. I wasn't here." I was in the damned underworld seeking information about my fated mate. Distracted from my duties, while my people suffered. The guilt nearly choked me. "But I could feel it. We need to ask the staff if they felt anything. Gather them in the main hall."

She nodded and ran off to sound the alarm, bringing Meralie with her. I heard her say something about getting the weeping woman a cup of tea, but I doubted that would help much.

My mind raced as I strode to the main hall. Six

demons had disappeared now. I was failing in my duty to protect them.

And Rathbine had something to do with it. I felt it in my gut.

It didn't take long for everyone to gather in the hall. There was a staff of over twenty who lived on the estate —housekeepers, cooks, security. It was well after midnight, so most were dressed in their sleepwear. Despite that, their gazes were alert and ready. I'd chosen every member of my staff for their quick reflexes and thinking. This estate was more than just a large house. It was the heart of my city—the shell that protected the Well of Souls.

And it was cracking.

I strode to the main staircase that swept toward the second floor and climbed the steps until everyone could see me. When I spoke, I made sure that my voice carried across the room. "Around eleven o'clock this morning, did anyone feel something strange near the Well of Souls? Think back. If you were in the part of the house that is nearest to the basement, you might have felt something."

There were murmurs through the crowd, then a small woman stepped forward. I recognized her as one of the cooks, and her eyes glinted with worry. "I thought I might have, yes. But I wrote it off as exhaustion. It was so brief I thought I'd made it up. Was I wrong to ignore it?"

Satisfaction and worry clashed inside of me. I didn't want anything to happen to the portal, but I was glad to have another clue about the string of disappearances. It appeared that the portal suffered some kind of power disruption whenever demons disappeared.

"No," I told her. "You couldn't have known. But if anyone feels it in the future, report directly to me or Liora."

There were nods and murmurs of assent, and the crowd parted. Liora joined me. "They're connected, aren't they?"

"I think so. I visited Rathbine just minutes ago, but he has an alibi."

"Doesn't mean he's not responsible."

"No, it doesn't. Though I did find him with three other Council members."

She grimaced. "Do you think they're in on it?"

"They could be."

"That's bad." Her grimace deepened. "It would be hard enough to get Rathbine. But multiple Council members? There's no way you'll get away with that, and the rest of the Council will come for us." She looked toward the people still drifting out of the hall, back to their beds. "They'll come for *them*."

I nodded, cold twisting through me. The Council knew where my heart lay. If I attacked any of them, they'd punish me the best way they knew how. And yet if I did nothing, my people would still suffer, disappearing to places unknown.

Cora

We were riding back to New Orleans when Fiona began to disappear again, her form flickering as her eyes widened with fear.

"Cora!" she cried, reaching for me.

I lunged for her, wrapping my arms around her waist, and holding tight. Like last time, unseen forces tried to drag her away from me.

"They're so strong," she cried, clinging tightly to me.

"What's happening?" Rei asked, panic in her voice.

"Help me hold onto her!" I shouted.

Rei and Mia grabbed Fiona. We piled together on one side of the car, holding on with all our might to our ephemeral friend. The forces that tugged at her were stronger than ever, and my skin went cold with fear.

I couldn't lose her.

And I owed her, after what my mother had done to her.

She clutched me like I was a lifeline, and I held on as hard as I could.

"What's going on?" the driver demanded.

We ignored him, focusing on Fiona. Finally, it stopped. Whatever was pulling on her let go, but we held on, breathing heavily as we huddled on top of Fiona.

"I think it's over," she gasped.

We pulled away, tumbling back onto our seats. She sat across from us, still fully visible and no longer flickering in and out of existence.

"Are you sure you're okay?" I asked.

She nodded shakily.

"All right, that's it. Get out." The cab driver opened his car door, and I realized that he'd stopped the vehicle.

I looked out the window. We were still several blocks from our houses. "We're not there yet."

He pulled open our door. "Don't care. No funny business in my car."

"It wasn't funny business," Mia insisted. "Our friend was being dragged away."

"That's even worse. I don't want to be dragged away, too."

"It doesn't work like that," I said, though I couldn't actually be sure.

"Still don't care. Get out." His voice was so hard that I obeyed. There was no point getting in a fight with a cab driver, especially since we were close to home.

My friends followed, and as soon as we were out on the street, the driver jumped back in the car and pulled away with a squeal of his tires.

"What the hell is going on?" Mia asked.

"I need a drink," Fiona said.

"Well, you can't have one," I said. "So what do you want instead?"

"To be home, I guess."

"Then let's go. We'll explain there," I said to Mia and Rei.

We tromped down the street in our party wear, and I wished we were stumbling back from a bar after a long night of fun.

My shop and apartment were quiet as we arrived, and we made our way up to the living space. I grabbed a bottle of wine and some coffee mugs, then collapsed on the couch with my friends.

"This is the second time Fiona has nearly disappeared," I said as I poured everyone a drink. "It's never happened before, though."

"That's not normal for ghosts, right?" Mia asked.

Fiona shook her head, her face twisted into a weird expression.

"What is it?" I asked, ignoring the wine I'd poured myself. "Is it happening again?"

"No, but I'm feeling...pulled somewhere. Not like before, where the invisible hands tried to yank me away from this plane. I feel like I'm being called to somewhere in town. Does that make sense?"

"Not really," I said. "Do you know where?"

"No. But I want to follow it." She stood and hurried

to the door, then turned back. "Well, come on. I can't go anywhere without you."

I set my cup down and followed her. Mia and Rei came along, but they didn't leave their cups. I didn't blame them. It had been a long night.

Fiona hurried down the stairs, silent and intent. It was almost like she was in a trance as she floated through town, passing bars filled with people and restaurants closed for the night. We passed late-night street musicians playing jazz and college kids going wild on Bourbon. But it wasn't until we neared Talan's estate that I realized where we were headed.

I hurried up alongside Fiona, catching her attention.

"Are you serious?" I asked.

She nodded, her gaze intent. "It's this direction that is calling to me. I *feel* it, Cora. I know it."

Shit. I hurried along beside her, hoping she would take a sharp left or right. Instead, she went right up to the guard house and tried to get onto the property. As before, she bounced off the protective charm.

"Damn it!" She spun to face me, her face twisted in an expression of angry frustration as she whispered, "I have to get in there!"

"Why?" Mia asked from beside me.

"I don't know." She shook her head frantically, trying to keep her voice low. "I just know there are answers there."

The guards who stood at the edge of the property

just stared at us, but I ignored them, my heart pounding. I had no idea what was going on, but the fact that Talan was involved...

Yeah, it was going to be a problem.

My gaze flicked to the guards. Could they hear what we were saying?

From the blank looks on their faces, I thought not. Fiona had tried to be quiet.

"Come on." I grabbed Fiona's arm and pulled her away. "We need to go discuss this somewhere else."

The others nodded, and we hurried back through town, leaving Talan's estate behind. I shot one last look over my shoulder before turning the corner. The guards still stared after us, and I was certain they'd report this to Talan. They hadn't heard what we'd said, but we'd certainly acted strange.

The street we'd turned onto was still alive with nightlife, golden streetlamps illuminating the partiers who spilled out of tiny bars and coffee shops. It was one of the cuter streets in New Orleans—a far cry from the insanity that was Bourbon.

My gaze snagged on a little coffee shop that was lit with a warm glow. I gesture toward it. "This way."

We headed toward the tiny building, which was delightfully called the Cozy Cup, and slipped inside the quirky interior. There were squashy armchairs everywhere, and a handwritten chalk sign advertising the cocktails that they served once evening hit. It was the smell of the coffee that got me, however.

"Sit wherever you like!" the barista called out from behind the counter. "We'll get your order at your table."

The tables were tiny little things positioned between clusters of comfy chairs. We found a spot in a quiet corner and huddled close together. A waitress appeared at our side within seconds, and we placed orders for coffee and cake. We might have some seriously dire stuff to discuss, but my stomach was rumbling.

Before she could return with our drinks, Rei jumped to her feet. "I'll be back in a few."

I frowned at her, but she was already out the door.

"That was weird," Mia said, then shrugged. "She's always been a bit odd, though."

As much as I wanted to know what was up with Rei, we had bigger things to worry about. I looked at Fiona. "Why were you drawn to Talan's estate?"

"I don't know." Worry creased her brow. "I just felt drawn to it. Like, it pulled me so hard I couldn't resist. It's still pulling."

"Not as hard as the force pulling you away from this plane, though," I said.

Her face paled. "No. Nothing pulls that hard." A shudder ran over her. "I didn't think I was going to be able to fight it that time. They almost got me."

"They?" Mia asked.

"I have no idea who," Fiona said. "Might not even be

real people. It just feels like hands—or a strong force—pulling me away. If it happens again, I think they might succeed."

"I've never heard of that happening to a ghost," Mia said.

"Me, neither." Fiona frowned. "Maybe we need to ask others if it's happening to them."

"Definitely," I said. "But we also need to figure out what the hell this has to do with Talan."

"There's something in his house," Fiona said. "I feel it. The force that pulls at me comes from there."

"Well, shit." I leaned back in the chair. "That's bad."

"No kidding." Mia nodded to the space behind me. "Coffee and cake are almost here."

I said nothing about Talan as the waitress delivered our food. Curls of steam rose from the coffee's surface, so I took a giant bite of chocolate cake to settle my nerves. It tasted divine—an explosion of cocoa and sugar and butter that made me want to shove the whole thing in my mouth.

I caught Fiona looking at the cake with longing and set down the fork. "It's pretty dry."

"Sure, Jan." She grinned. "Thanks, though."

I nodded. "So, we need to get into Talan's house and investigate."

"What if he's behind all this?" Mia asked.

I frowned. I was mad as hell at him for lying to me

about the mate thing, and he was definitely overbearing and ruthless—but this?

It was too much.

Right?

"I don't know if he would do something so terrible," I said. But how did I know that? How *could* I know that? All we had between us was attraction and one wild kiss. And he *had* lied to me about the whole fated mate thing. That was kind of a huge deal. I barely knew him. "But the problem *is* coming from his basement."

"So we don't know if he's responsible, which means we can't tell him exactly what's going on," Mia said.

"And I can't sneak in there," Fiona said. "At least not without breaking through the protective charm that keeps the unseen out."

"That charm is going to be strong." Mia frowned. "I don't think it's possible to break."

"So we have to find a way to get you invited in," I said. "Then you need to be able to get away and snoop around."

Fiona nodded. "Yep. Sounds about right."

"So I've got to distract him." A shiver of anticipation ran over me. Fear, too. Just a little bit. Until I knew more about him, it was only smart to be wary.

The door to the cafe opened, and Rei hurried back inside. Her cheeks were flushed and her hair wild. She'd changed from her heels into running shoes, and she'd clearly raced through town to get back here.

"Where were you?" Mia asked.

Rei collapsed into a chair, panting slightly. She held up two bracelets. "I had to go get these."

"What are they?"

"They're a pair. They link life forces. Fiona might be a ghost, but she still has a life force, though it's weaker than ours. Anyway, if she gets sucked away again, it will be harder for her get taken if someone else is wearing a bracelet that links their life force to hers."

I held out a hand for one of the bracelets. "Give it over."

"I haven't told you the downside yet," she said.

I shrugged. "Don't really care. She's my friend."

The first real friend I'd ever had. Certainly, my best friend, even though we'd only known each other a short time.

Fiona swallowed hard, her eyes glinting with unshed tears.

"When the forces try to pull Fiona away from this plane, your life force will help bind her here," Rei said. "But if they keep pulling or get stronger, they could eventually take you with her."

Made sense, and I wasn't surprised to hear her say it. But I kept my hand extended and made a grabbing motion. "Hand it over."

She nodded and did as I asked, and I clipped the little leather and silver bracelet on. She put the matching one on Fiona, and it immediately turned transparent as it touched her skin.

"I wish you could do this with dresses," she said, her voice slightly teary through her laugh.

"It takes way too much magic. But I'll work on it," Rei said. "You never know."

Fiona threw her arms around her and squeezed, then lunged for me and hugged so hard that she'd have crushed me if she hadn't been a ghost.

"Thank you," she said. "You're a million times better than I thought you were when you first showed up."

I laughed at the memory of her throwing books at me, but my heart squeezed at the predicament we were in. If I lost her...

I didn't even want to think about it.

6

Cora

The next morning, I woke early to get started on solving the Fiona problem. I'd been too exhausted last night, nearly staggering with exhaustion. Fiona had dragged me back to the house, and I'd collapsed in the bed. Balthazar had jumped onto my butt and curled up, and it was the last thing I remembered.

But today was a new day, and I was going to save my friend.

I showered quickly, then threw on jeans and a T-shirt and pulled my hair up. Fiona was waiting in the kitchen with Balthazar, who was once again curled up on top of the toaster. It was turned to the hottest setting and cooking away. He purred like mad.

"Don't tell me he got that toaster up here by himself," I said.

She shook her head. "He's been having trouble with the uphill portion of the stairs, so I helped him."

"Good of you." I'd never be able to eat toast again, but that was fine. Balthazar got far more joy out of that toaster than I ever would. "I'm headed out to figure out what the hell is going on. You're coming, right?"

"Wouldn't miss it." She hopped off the counter and followed me down the stairs and through the bookshop.

The morning was unusually cool, and I took it as a good sign. "We're going to figure this out," I said, glad to hear that I sounded peppy.

"But first you need coffee."

I looked at her. "Do I look that bad?"

"I call it like I see it."

I grinned. I probably looked exhausted, since it had been a late night, but she wasn't wrong. I *did* need coffee. As we crossed the street toward Mia's cafe, Fiona faded until she was nearly invisible. She was still trying to maintain a low profile when we were out, primarily for my benefit. I didn't need people to know about my power over the dead, and she was good enough to keep that in mind.

Fortunately, there was no one in Mia's place, so she reappeared when we entered.

Mia grinned as she saw us, then turned to the coffee pot on the back counter and poured a go-cup of coffee.

"Headed to the demon lord's place?" she asked, passing the cup over the counter along with a bagel filled with cream cheese.

"Yep."

I reached into my pocket for cash, and she scowled at me. "Don't even think about it."

"You run a business!"

"It's a day-old bagel. I think I can afford to lose it."

I grinned. "Thanks, you're the best."

I was still fairly broke, given that I hadn't yet managed to get the shop up and running. I'd taken to coming by in the evening to help Mia clean up—mostly so we could hang out—but the positive result was that she gave me breakfast the next morning. I had a feeling she'd do it anyway, so I made it a point to get over here in the evenings to help out. It was a win-win for me, since I got to hang out with a friend.

It was still weird to have them, and there was a huge part of me that wanted to hide away in my house and avoid people—old habits die hard—but I was working on becoming a more normal, well-rounded person.

After saying goodbye, Fiona and I headed back outside. She faded once again, but I could feel her presence as we made our way toward the demon lord's estate. I polished off the bagel in record time and downed the coffee. We were halfway there when a thought occurred to me.

I looked at Fiona's nearly invisible form. "What if this is affecting more ghosts than just you?"

She frowned. "Good point. We should ask."

I nodded. "Let me find one."

"You can find us?"

I shrugged. "Same way I can bring you with me places, I guess. My magic is weird."

"Well, get to it then."

I grinned, then focused on my power. It only took me a moment to get a read on someone in the old grocery store to our right.

"There." I pointed and turned toward the door.

"This place? Really?" Fiona followed me into the quaint interior.

It was tiny and cramped, but meticulously clean. The shelves were stocked with specialty items that made my mouth water—wine and fancy crackers, chocolates and cookies. But it was the cold case along the right wall that caught my eye. The assortment of cheeses was enough to make my head spin.

"Wow," Fiona whispered. "I stand corrected. This place is amazing."

I nodded to the young guy behind the counter. He had a magnificent hipster mustache and a pair of pale-yellow sunglasses that shielded his eyes. He gave me the chin tip that so many younger guys were fond of, and I turned into the stacks of delicacies to look for the ghost.

I walked toward the back, where I was feeling the

strongest signature, and ran my gaze over the goods on the shelf. If I ever had a decent amount of money, I'd be coming back here. Screw fancy clothes or electronics—this was where happiness lived.

At the back of the shop was the freezer section—a magnificent array of small ice cream containers in every flavor I could imagine. I dragged my gaze away and looked at the far back corner of the shop.

An empty chair sat there, completely out of place in the otherwise perfectly organized store.

"They're over there?" Fiona whispered at my side.

"You can't sense them?"

"No. I'm just regular dead, not the kind that has death powers."

"Well, they're over there. Not wanting to show themselves." Not that it would stop me. I called upon my power, letting it rise to the surface. "Show yourself."

"No." The grumpy voice came from the chair, but I still couldn't see them.

I could feel the ghost's resistance and pushed harder with my power. "We aren't going to bother you. We just have a few questions."

"Ugh. Fine."

I wasn't sure if it was my power or the ghost's willingness to show herself, but an old woman appeared in the chair, one leg propped over the other, a cigarette smoking lazily in her hand.

She wore clothing from another decade—the

eighties, I was pretty sure—and her fluffy, transparent hair had once been white. She had to have died some time in her nineties, and she somehow managed to look both grumpy and like a kindly grandmother.

"You can't smoke in here," Fiona blurted.

"Honey, I'm dead. I can do whatever I want." She pointed her cigarette at Fiona. "You should try to remember that yourself."

"And what you want is to haunt this old grocery store?" Fiona asked.

She nodded toward the front, where the young guy managed the counter. "Got to make sure my great-grandson keeps the place running how I like, now don't I?"

Ah, so she used to own the little shop. It now made sense why she was back here, smoking in the ice cream aisle.

"Now, what was your question?" she asked. "I haven't got all day. My break is almost over."

"Over the last two days, have you ever felt yourself being pulled away from this plane?" I asked.

Fiona leaned forward, adding, "Like hands are grabbing you and trying to tear you away."

The woman frowned. "How do you know about that?"

"It's been happening to me," Fiona said. "We're wondering if it's happening to others."

"Well, it is." The old woman scowled. "Happened to Myrtle across the road, too."

"Myrtle?" I asked.

"Ghost at the hair salon. Keeping an eye on her great niece."

I heaved out a frustrated sigh. At least three ghosts were affected, probably more. "Thank you for your help."

"You going to fix it?" she asked.

"I'm going to try."

She nodded. "Good. I didn't like it."

"That's an understatement," Fiona said. "It's the *worst.*"

For both of us. I still remembered the cold fear I'd experienced when I'd thought I was going to lose her. "Let's get out of here. We need to figure this out ASAP."

Fiona nodded, then waved at the ghost and disappeared. I felt her presence as she followed me out of the grocery store, and we hurried toward the demon lord's estate.

We'd only gone two blocks when I felt the telltale prickle of someone watching me. My skin chilled, but my step didn't falter. I couldn't let them know I was onto them.

But Fiona seemed to sense my unease and whispered, "Is anything wrong?"

"I think we're being followed. Can you check it out?"

I felt her presence disappear and continued down

the street. That was one of the major pros of having a ghost friend. She could look for a tail without anyone realizing it was happening.

It only took a minute for her to return. She leaned close to whisper, "We're being followed by a man with mousy brown hair and glasses. He looks like an accountant."

"Shit." I knew exactly who it was. It was one of my old boss's goons. He was excellent at tailing people because he looked so average and benign. He was anything but. He should've known better than to wear his usual disguise around me, though. I would recognize him in a heartbeat.

"Okay, slight change of plan. Just going to take a short little diversion." I pulled out my phone, as if it were ringing, and put it to my ear. "Hello?"

I didn't know if the goon was close enough to hear, but details matter. I carried on a conversation as I approached an alley. I ducked into it like I was trying to get away from the noise of the street and stood with my back to the entrance. I kept the phone pressed to my ear as I whispered to Fiona, "Wait at the entrance of the alley, okay? Let me know when he's almost here."

"Gotcha." Fiona's presence disappeared.

I waited, senses on overdrive, as I pulled my knife from the ether. I held it in front of me so that my attacker wouldn't be able to see it.

A moment later, Fiona's whisper carried to me. "Almost here."

I hummed into the phone, as if I were responding to something that someone had said and listened closely for footsteps behind me. I didn't hear him approach, but I felt the air shift subtly around me. It wasn't a physical thing, more like a knowledge that I was no longer alone.

I knew how I would handle this if I were him, and I was ninety-nine percent sure he would do it the same way. We had been raised at the same orphanage, after all, and had learned the same techniques.

When I felt his hand grip the back of my arm, I spun and slammed my fist into his jaw. He stumbled backward, and I took advantage of his surprise, slamming him against the brick wall of the alley, and pressed my blade to his throat. Shock widened his brown eyes, then his mouth tightened with fear.

"Come now, Freddy. Did you really think you could sneak up on me?"

"The master has a message for you."

"I'm sure that's not all he has for me." I raised a brow. "Or were you not sent to bring me back?"

I could see the truth in his eyes. Freddie knew what I was capable of, and he carried a pair of anti-magic cuffs in his hand. He'd planned to snap them on me so I couldn't use my power against him, and then drag me back to captivity.

No way in hell would I let that happen.

"You expect me to kill you right?" I asked.

He nodded, looking like he wanted to faint. Obviously, I should kill him. Any decent mercenary would. Eliminate the threat, continue surviving: our two most sacred rules.

However, I wasn't a mercenary anymore. I had never wanted to be, and now that I was free, I wouldn't continue down the path they'd forced on me when I was young.

"Here's the thing, Freddy. I don't have it in me. I never did." I pressed the blade to his throat hard enough to make a shallow cut. I didn't want him to stop fearing me, however. I needed that fear. "I've got a new life now, and I'm going to keep living it. I'll let you keep living yours if you leave me the hell alone."

He nodded frantically, and I wasn't sure I could believe him. But I also couldn't kill him—especially since we came from the same place. Freddy liked the lifestyle, and he would never try to leave, but what if he hadn't been taken to the orphanage as a child? Would he have grown up to actually be an accountant, instead of a mercenary who dressed like one?

Maybe.

I would use my powers if I absolutely had to, and this wasn't that scenario. I reached down and yanked the anti-magic cuffs from Freddy. They were incredibly valuable, and I knew that my old boss only had two pairs. It had taken him years to acquire them. If Freddy didn't have them, he was far less likely to approach me. And hell, they would probably come in handy one day.

"I'm going to step back and give you a chance to run," I said, my voice cold and hard. "If you don't, and you try to attack me, I will kill you."

Freddie nodded again, and I could see in his eyes that he was going to do as I told him.

I stepped back, keeping the blade raised in front of me. He turned and ran, sprinting down the alley and out of sight.

Fiona appeared at my side. "Whew. That was close."

"Not as close as it could've been. Thank you for your help."

"Want to tell me about it?"

"Maybe one day." Fiona knew a little bit about my power, but she didn't really know anything about my past. I wanted to keep it that way. For one, I was ashamed of the work I'd been forced to do. I tried my best not to kill unless I knew the person was truly evil, but I wished I'd escaped sooner. Anyway, I didn't want to revisit that past, even in conversation. I had a new life, and I was a new person.

"Let's go." I tucked the anti-magic cuffs in my pocket and headed back out onto Main Street. Fiona followed.

We walked in silence toward the demon lord's home, but I felt Fiona staying close to my side. I appreciated it.

My heart began to race as we neared the estate, memories of Talan filling my mind. I was still angry at him—of course I was—but I couldn't help but want to see him.

Ugh. I was weak.

"So, how are you planning to get me in?" Fiona asked. "Because I still can't enter without his permission."

"I'm going to go up to the gate and tell the guards that both of us want to talk to him. He'll let us in."

"How do you know?"

I thought of the way he looked at me—all that heat and intensity—then shot Fiona a bemused glance. "Really?"

"Oh, right. The whole mate thing. Yeah, he'll let us in." She paused. "But how will you explain that I'm with you when ghosts usually can't go far from the place they died?"

"I'll say you're a special ghost." I raised the bracelet I now wore. "And that this helps."

"You think he'll buy it?"

"Do we have a choice?"

"Good point. Then what?"

"As soon as we're in, you disappear and go exploring. I'll cover for you. Say you're invisible or something and then distract him."

"It's as good as anything, I guess."

"It's a *great* plan."

She laughed. "Sure, sure." She frowned. "But what if I can't be too far away from you?"

"We'll be in the same building, so it will probably be fine. If not, we'll figure it out."

We were only a couple blocks from Talan's place when Fiona said, "I can feel that we're going in the right direction. It's at his estate for sure."

I wasn't thrilled to hear it, but I also wasn't surprised. That was why we were here, after all. Just because I didn't want him to be responsible for my friend's disappearance didn't mean he was innocent.

We reached the end of the street that led up to his property and stopped.

"Yep. It's coming from there," Fiona said.

I stared at the massive iron wall and impressive home beyond. Two guards in identical uniforms stood at the entrance. They stared at us suspiciously.

I didn't give them a single thought, however. I couldn't, not as long as Talan was in my head. The thought of him made my heart thunder like mad, a pounding that nearly made me lightheaded.

"You, okay?" Fiona whispered.

"Yeah. Totally fine. I should be worried about you."

"Nah. I'm tough." She squeezed my shoulder, a comforting gesture that felt a bit weird due to her ephemeral nature.

"Let's go." I crossed the street and stopped at the gate, shooting the guards a cheeky grin. It was probably a bit manic and definitely wasn't my normal style, but I needed them to be a little off guard.

They frowned, and I said to Fiona, "Might as well show yourself."

She did as I asked, and the guards' frowns deepened. They approached the open gate and blocked our way.

I stopped a few feet from them. "We would like to see the demon lord. I'm Cora, and this is Fiona."

"The Unseen can't enter the property."

"Well, you can see her now."

"Still, she could disappear, and then there would be trouble."

I heaved a sigh. "Just call him and tell him that Cora wants to see him, but I'll only come in if I can bring my friend."

They grumbled to each other. I caught snippets of their conversation, and it was clear they wanted to tell me that there was no way Talan would let us in if Fiona was coming along.

"Just do it," Fiona said. "He'll be pissed if you don't tell him I'm here, I guarantee it."

Something in her voice must have convinced them, because the one on the left turned and went to the guard house. A few minutes later, he stalked back toward us with a grimace. "You're welcome to enter. Both of you."

"Thanks."

"But I'll be escorting you."

"Fine by me." It wasn't ideal, but we'd manage.

Fiona and I stepped across the boundary and

headed down the path. I ignored the guard who stuck close to us and whispered to Fiona, "Might as well go for it."

She nodded and began to fade.

"What's going on?" The guard demanded. "She shouldn't be disappearing."

"It's what ghosts do," I said. "She's still here."

"How can you guarantee it?"

"She's still here, I promise." She totally wasn't. I'd felt it as soon as she'd left us, clearly moving as fast as she could toward the basement.

The guard grumbled, but I ignored him as I walked toward Talan's house. The garden was as insanely beautiful and creepy as ever, with the vibrant flowers and butterflies that turned it into a wonderland. We passed the little creek on the right, where the alligator stared at me with bulbous eyes.

I shivered. As a city girl, I was still *real* uncomfortable around alligators. Fortunately, we reached the house without the gator following us, and I went straight to the door of his office and knocked.

7

Fiona

As I left Cora, my heart raced, excitement surging through me.

I'm on my own.

For the first time since I'd died, I was on my own out in the world. The four walls of the bookstore had been feeling claustrophobic for weeks. And while I loved going around town with Cora, there was just something about being on my own that felt amazing. I needed to do this more often.

I didn't mind being a ghost so much—there was something peaceful about it. As if my mind were quieter in this state. But getting a taste of real life again made me want more of it.

Drifting through Talan's garden definitely qualified as *more*. It was amazing here—a garden out of my wildest fantasies, and a few nightmares. The large green snakes that hung from one of the trees watched me with eerie black eyes. Frankly, right now, I was grateful to be dead. They couldn't touch me in this state.

When the massive hell hounds ran up to me, their eyes blazing with fire, it took everything I had not to flinch backward.

They can't hurt me.

And it seemed they didn't want to. When they reached me, they sat on their fluffy butts, tongues lolling, and grinned at me.

"Hey, guys," I murmured. "Do you like me because I'm dead?"

They kept grinning, and I wanted to pet them. I didn't really have time to dawdle, but they were just so damned cute. I took a moment to rub each one on the head, then hurried toward the house.

When I reached it, I floated right through the exterior wall, following the dark magic that pulled at me. Whatever it was, it was new. I'd never felt anything so terrible coming from here. True, I hadn't visited often, but my recent visit with Cora had been devoid of this awful darkness in the air. It made my skin crawl.

Quickly, I floated through the halls of Talan's magnificent house. It was absolutely gorgeous, but there was no time to inspect it more closely. I had to discover the source of the magic that pulsed so malevolently.

When I found the locked wooden door at the back of the house, a shiver ran over me. This was it. For sure.

I drifted through the wood and down the stairs. The dark magic grew stronger as I descended, making my stomach turn and my skin chill—even though I didn't even have real skin anymore. It was crazy how the magic made me feel more alive and yet, more threatened at the same time.

I reached the basement, slowing my forward progress as the magic became thicker and more offensive. I breathed shallowly through my mouth, drifting toward the power that called to me. Every inch of me screamed to back away—to get out of here. And yet, I couldn't seem to help myself.

It had gotten me in its grasp, and it wouldn't let go.

Talan

As soon as I heard the knock on the door, my heart raced. I resisted rubbing my chest and scowled.

Calex looked at me, his brows raised.

I glared at him, then went to the door and pulled it

open. Cora stood on the other side, and my heart rate only increased. It was damned irritating.

But she was alone. And so beautiful it made my chest hurt. There was such strength in her that I found myself drawn to it.

I moved to the right to let her enter.

Cora stepped inside, giving me a wide berth that made my chest ache even more. She didn't want to be anywhere near me.

Good.

I knew it was a lie even as I thought it. I despised lies, even ones I told myself. But I didn't have the will to face something as obnoxious as emotions. Not now.

Not ever.

She smiled at Calex, and I felt jealousy seethe inside me.

"Where's your friend?" I asked.

"She's here," Cora said. "Just invisible."

"Invisible?"

"It weakens her to travel like this."

"She must be a rare type of ghost to be able to leave the place of her death," Calex said.

She raised her wrist to indicate a bracelet I'd never seen her wear before. "This allows her to follow me. And we're here because we have a problem."

"Are you here because the demon lord is breaking the law?" she asked him.

"No, though he might be. You can never tell with

him." Calex shot her a smile. The golden bastard was really turning on the charm.

With my mate.

The possessiveness roared inside me.

I stepped back, clenching my fists to regain control of myself. It was a physiological thing for demons to become possessive of their mates, but I wouldn't let it rule me. *I* was in control of myself, not fate.

The door burst open behind Cora. I moved without thinking, getting between her and the threat.

Liora, my second, stood in the doorway, panting. Calex shot me a knowing look, but I ignored him.

"Another one?" I asked.

She nodded. "Two more disappearances. Just now. I got word from the guards."

"Damn it." The curse ripped from me.

"Disappearances?" Cora asked. "What's going on?"

"Demons are going missing," I said. "Magically, I mean. They're here one moment, then poof, they're gone. That's why Calex is here. We're trying to get to the bottom of it."

She paled. "How many demons? Where are they going?"

"Nearly ten now, and we don't know." I leaned against the bookshelf behind me, pinching the bridge of my nose. *Ten* of my people. Gone.

"And they're disappearing at different times?" she asked.

"In groups." I frowned at her. "Why are you so interested?"

"Can't I be interested in my own town?"

"Yes, but it's more than that."

She looked from Calex to me, the wheels clearly turning behind her eyes. She was debating how much information to trust me with, and I was suddenly desperate to know whatever she had come here to say.

"I'm not—"

Fiona appeared, cutting off Cora's words. She materialized a few feet away from her friend, her expression terrified.

"We've got to go." Fiona lunged for Cora and grabbed her arm. Magic pulsed on the air. A moment later, they were gone.

I blinked, dumbfounded.

"That shouldn't be possible," Liora said.

"No, it shouldn't be." My house was guarded from ether transport without the use of portals, and yet, somehow Cora and Fiona had managed it.

But which one had controlled it? And where had they gone?

~

Cora

. . .

The ether spun me through space and spat me out in the middle of my bookstore. I staggered toward the desk and leaned against it, trying to catch my breath. Traveling through the ether was intense enough when one was expecting it. An unexpected journey was enough to make me want to puke.

I looked up at Fiona. "What did you find that scared you so bad? And how the hell did you do that?"

"One, I have no idea how I did that." She looked as shocked as I felt. "And whatever is making me disappear, it's in his basement." She shuddered. "He's responsible."

"I'm not so sure." I thought back to the short conversation we'd had. He hadn't mentioned the portal when we'd spoken about the disappearances, but he hadn't had time.

"What are you thinking?" Fiona asked.

"Demons are going missing," I said. "Possibly at the same time you're feeling pulled away from this plane."

"And you think they're connected."

"I do. Especially if the events are happening at the same time."

"But why would the demon lord hurt his own people?"

"He wouldn't." I didn't like his lying about the whole mate thing, but I knew that much about him. "He brought Calex in to help him figure out what's going wrong."

"Do you think he knows about what's happening to the ghosts?"

I shook my head. "I don't think so."

Fiona grimaced. "So, I might have pulled you out of there too soon."

"No, it's fine. Always go with your gut. We can go back and talk to him."

A knock sounded at the door, and I frowned. Who the hell would be visiting me?

I strode toward the door and pulled it open.

Talan stood there.

Of course.

"Why did you leave so quickly?" he demanded.

"Why did you immediately hunt me down?" I countered. "You got here in no time at all."

"I was worried about you."

Damn. Maybe my question had been unfair. "We're fine. But we'd like to know what the hell is in your basement."

In the past, I would have played my cards closer to the vest. But I trusted him not to hurt his own people. Whatever was in his basement wasn't bad because of something he'd done.

He frowned, then his gaze flicked toward Fiona. "You were never in my office, were you?"

She shook her head.

"Clever," he said. "Can I come inside?"

I stepped aside so he could enter, and he slipped by

me. I closed the door and turned around, waiting for his explanation.

"The portal in my basement leads to the underworld that I—and most of the demons in New Orleans—came from. It's powered by a little piece of each of our souls, which is why it's called the Well of Souls."

Shit, that had to be some seriously powerful magic. "And it's malfunctioning?"

He nodded. "We believe it's been tampered with. That portal is what allows every demon in my part of New Orleans to live here without being bound to another magical creature."

"It's your freedom."

"Essentially. It creates a part of the world where demons can live."

"Does it have any impact on ghosts?" I asked.

"Why?

"Fiona is being impacted, I think."

He nodded. "It makes sense. My part of town does have more ghosts than any other. We think the portal allows more of them to stay on this plane, just like it allows the demons."

"So, when it malfunctions, it affects me too," Fiona said.

"Precisely," he said.

I met Fiona's gaze. She seemed to be buying it. I was, too. It made sense.

"Why would someone tamper with it?" I asked.

"It's the only portal of its kind in the world, and its capabilities are endless."

Suddenly, I understood. "Someone else wants their own piece of Earth, and they're willing to get rid of all your demons to get it, aren't they?"

"That's our theory. We want to talk to the witnesses first. See if there were any clues from those who disappeared that might point us in the right direction."

"I'll help."

He nodded. "Thank you. Calex is already out canvassing."

"Good. Give me some names, and I'll hit the pavement."

8

Cora

"I can't believe you insisted on going with me." I shot him a look out of the corner of my eye. He towered over me, so it was hard to see his expression, but I had a feeling it was set in stone.

"We work better as a team," he said.

I agreed with him—we'd found the kidnapped women last week--but didn't want to admit it. So I just grunted.

I picked up the pace, determined to get this over with. Almost immediately, I remembered that I didn't know where we were going. "Where is this guy?"

"We're almost there. He lives two blocks up, above

the old movie theater. His wife went missing earlier today."

My heart hurt for the guy. I'd never had a real partner before, and I couldn't even imagine what it would feel like to lose them so unexpectedly. It had to be horrible. I shoved the thoughts from my mind and focused on the task at hand. Getting caught up in emotions wouldn't do me any good.

The streets were busier in this part of town, restaurants and art galleries full of tourists out for a day in the sun. But it wasn't hard to find the old movie theater. It was one of those ornate places, probably from the 1920s. The old whiteboard had the usual black letters spelling out the latest movies. The bare bulbs that surrounded it would sparkle prettily at night.

Right now, though, the place was dead empty.

I looked up toward the windows on the second story. They were open to the warm breeze, and I could hear the sound of crying inside. I looked at Talan. "Does the missing demon have children?"

"A teenage daughter."

"Shit." My determination to figure out the cause of the disappearances increased. I knew what it was like to grow up without a mother. I didn't want that for anybody.

Talan led the way to the side door that bypassed the movie theater. We ascended a dark narrow staircase that led to a surprisingly open and airy foyer. Two doors led off the open space, and he turned to the one marked "Apartment 1B." He raised his hand to knock, but before he could make contact, the door swung open.

A tired-looking man stood on the other side, his short horns peeking through his curly hair. Gray edged the temples, but it was the exhaustion that made him look old. "You came." He dragged a hand through his hair. "Thank you so much. To have the demon lord himself... It means a lot."

"May we come in?" Talan's voice was softer and kinder than I'd ever heard it before. I felt my brows rise.

The man nodded and stepped aside. Talan walked to the door, and I followed. The apartment was a homey, pretty place. Large windows provided the view over the street, and the walls were painted a warm burnt orange. The mismatched furniture was eclectic and lovely, but it was the girl on the corner of the sofa who caught my eye. She wept into the sleeve of her sweatshirt, mascara smeared around her eyes.

"Have a seat." The man gestured to the two arm chairs directly opposite the sofa.

I took a seat, but I wanted to sit next to the girl and wrap my arm around her shoulders. The desire to comfort was the strangest instinct for me. I hadn't felt it much in my life, probably because I'd spent the majority of my time with people who would throw me under a bus without a second thought.

But I felt it now, and it was like an ill-fitting shirt.

Talan sat and propped his arms on his knees. "Can you tell us what happened?"

"It was about two hours ago." The man raked his hand through his hair again, a nervous tick that was going into overdrive. "One minute, Kathy was sitting right here. The next, there was a powerful pulse of magic, and she was gone."

The girl on the couch gave a ragged sob.

I couldn't take it anymore. I rose from my chair and went to sit next to her. Close enough that she would know I was there, but not so close as to make it weird. She scrubbed the sleeves of her sweatshirt over her face and turned to look at me. "Who are you?"

"I'm Cora. I'm here to help find your mom."

"How are you qualified?"

Teenagers. I didn't know much about them, but this seemed right in line with what to expect. I gave a smile. "Not sure I am that qualified. But I'm good at finding things, and I know how to kick ass."

She gave a watery smile. "Lame."

I laughed. It was hard to impress teenagers. But at least I got a smile out of her. "Is there anything you remember about your mother's disappearance?"

"I thought I smelled sulfur." She shrugged. "Could be wrong, though."

I frowned and looked at Talan. "Sulfur? Have you heard that from anybody else?"

"No, but we'll start asking." He pulled out his phone and typed a message, presumably to Calex.

"There have been more disappearances?" the man asked.

"A few," Talan said. "I know this isn't what you signed up for when you moved here. But we're going to figure it out and get your wife back."

The man gave a weary sigh, and his hands inevitably returned to his hair, driving the furrows deeper. "I know that. Trust me, I'm grateful for everything you've done. We knew there were risks when we came here, but it's been worth it." The respect and appreciation in his eyes were unmistakable. So was the hope.

It made me shift uncomfortably in my seat. Hope always made me nervous. I didn't want to let these people down. Hell, I didn't want to let Fiona down. I couldn't. I owed her after what my mother had done to her, and I didn't want to lose her.

"Was there anything else?" I leaned toward the man, trying to instill the importance of the question into my voice. "Anything at all that you can remember, no matter how small."

He frowned, his expression going distant. "It happened so fast. But when I tried to grab her, it felt like somebody was pulling her from around the waist."

That was roughly how Fiona had described it. Whatever was happening to her was the exact same thing happening to the demons.

"Thank you," Talan said. "We appreciate the help. We'll keep you informed."

"Aren't the police working on this, too?" the girl asked.

"Yes," Talan said. "Their chief detective is currently questioning another family. We'll compare notes to get to the bottom of this."

The man turned to his daughter. "We're lucky to have the demon lord himself looking into this. You're too young to remember what life was like before we came here, but we owe everything to him. It took strength and genius to build this place for us in New Orleans. When it comes to finding your mother, he's the best person for the job."

The girl nodded, but I could still see the doubt in her eyes. I didn't blame her.

"Thank you," she said. "I appreciate it."

Her father nodded approvingly.

We rose to go, and he escorted us to the door. He thanked Talan again, and soon we were on the other side. I looked up at Talan. "Sulfur?"

"It's often a scent in the underworld," he said. "Perhaps that's where they're going. It's the most likely thing."

"That's where demons go when they die, but in this scenario, too?"

"Could be. Let's head to the next family and see what

they have to say." He paused. "I wonder if Fiona has smelled sulfur as well."

I shivered. It was terrible for demons to be taken unwillingly back to their underworld, but at least they were familiar with the place. If Fiona was dragged to a demon underworld, she would be in serious trouble.

"Let's go." I headed down the stairs and out onto the brightly lit street.

Talan led the way to the next house. This time, it was a missing roommate, a young man, thirty years old and single. His roommate described the circumstances of his disappearance in almost the exact same terms that the first man had. Otherwise, there were no connections between them, beside their species.

At the next apartment, we heard roughly the same description of events from a twenty-five-year-old woman who had lost her boyfriend. As we were leaving her building, I looked up at Talan. "What do you want to bet that Calex has found exactly the same things we have?"

"I'm not taking that bet." He turned down the street, heading toward my house.

"Was that the last family?"

"Yes. Calex spoke to the others, with the help of a detective." He pulled out his phone and typed a quick message.

I waited for the response to come through, my mind still spinning. A moment later, the phone dinged. Talan read the message and said, "He can meet us at your place in ten minutes. He's finished, too."

At the bookshop, I found Fiona waiting for us. She sat on the checkout desk, her legs swinging. Balthazar sat next to her, curled up on his trusty toaster. Her expression brightened when she saw us. "Have you figured it out?"

Guilt tugged at me. I didn't have nearly the number of answers she wanted. "We're closer. Is there any chance you've smelled sulfur when you were being dragged away?"

She frowned. "Sulfur? Maybe? It was very faint. I just knew that everything smelled terrible and felt terrible. Like I was being taken to the worst place in the world."

Yep. That would describe a demon underworld from the perspective of a human.

She frowned. "Why do you ask?"

"The others smelled it as well, but they were demons."

A knock sounded on the door behind us, then it was slowly pushed open. Calex stepped through. He gave us a weary smile. "Let me guess. Everyone disappeared in roughly the same fashion, and they smelled sulfur."

"Correct for $800, Calex," I said.

"I have no idea what you mean by that," Talan said.

"It's a *Jeopardy* reference," Calex said. "As the demon lord, I don't imagine you have a lot of time to watch gameshows."

Talan made a low noise of agreement in his throat. "From what we've heard so far, there seems to be no connection, other than species."

"Don't forget ghosts," Fiona said. "This has been happening to others, not just me."

My phone buzzed in my pocket. I pulled it out and read the text from Rei, which was perfectly timed. "Rei has asked around in her neighborhood. None of the ghosts who live in the witch's part of town have had a problem."

Talan frowned. "So it's a problem in our area alone."

"Do you have any thoughts about who might be screwing with your portal?" I asked.

"I think it's Rathbine, someone I used to know in my underworld. He's always coveted this part of New Orleans."

"Then let's go get them!" Fiona jumped off the desk.

"I wish it were that easy," Talan said. "Demons have a Council that oversees us. There are a dozen members, twelve of the most powerful demons in the world. I'm on the Council, but so is our suspect. If I act against him, it's a declaration of war against the entire group. And since they know that the most important thing to me is my people, they would go after them first."

Fiona heaved a dejected sigh and leaned against the desk. "So, we're going to have to be sneaky. Normally, I would be into that, but I really want to fix this fast."

"I understand that." Once again, Talan's tone was soft

and soothing. I stared at him, surprised by the many facets of the demon lord who was giving me so much trouble.

"I promise we're going to fix this as fast as we can," he said. "But we need irrefutable proof that it's him before we attack. Otherwise, we'll cause more damage than good."

"How are you going to get proof?" Calex asked. "I saw the portal. There's no visible sign of tampering."

"What about something we can't see?" I asked.

The three others turned to me.

"When I lived in New York, there was a witch who specialized in spells that could reveal hidden magic. Maybe she can help us."

Talan nodded slowly, his expression thoughtful. "I like this idea. There's no question that magic was used to manipulate the portal into malfunctioning. If we can get evidence of what kind of magic it was, I'll have enough to take out Rathbine."

"Can we see her today?" Calex asked.

I looked at Fiona, worry twisting my heart. "We're going to have to."

9

Cora

It was damned unfortunate that the witch, Ophelia, refused to leave New York. To make matters worse, she only made deals in person.

The idea of going back to the city made an iron fist tighten around my heart and cold dread streak up my spine. I had vowed never to return. Yet here I was, not even a month later, rolling back into the city.

Well, not rolling exactly. We didn't have to drive, thanks to Talan. The demon lord had access to a portal that would take us nearly all the way to Ophelia's place. When I'd heard how close we could get, I was a little bit relieved.

Ophelia lived on a quiet, tree-lined street of brownstone townhouses. Her type of magic was profitable, and she liked to live well. The fact that her neighbors were mostly human was a good thing as far as I was concerned. I didn't think my old boss had a spell set up to detect when I returned to the city, but if he did, I wanted to stay as far away from the magical parts of New York as possible.

"Are you all right?" Talan asked as soon as we stepped out of the portal and into the quiet alley in New York.

I looked up at him, wondering what he could see in me that made him ask. "Yeah, fine."

"I haven't known you long, but you're obviously tense."

"Just not a fan of the city." Shit, that was a stupid thing to say. "And I'm worried about Fiona. I really like her."

"She's lucky to have you on her side." His gaze stayed on my face, piercing the heart of me. Could he see more than he let on?

Yes. I didn't know how, but yes.

I turned away and headed toward the main street. "Let's go. If Ophelia isn't home, we'll have to look for her and that will take a while."

Talan joined me, staying close to my side as we walked down the once familiar street. I'd be lying if I said I didn't appreciate his proximity. My old boss would think twice about approaching me if Talan were at my side.

We reached Ophelia's house a minute later. I'd come here frequently for help with my jobs, and she'd been one of my secret weapons in being the most effective mercenary in New York. I knocked on the door and waited anxiously. The flowers in the window boxes had changed since I'd been there last, and I focused on them instead of thoughts of my old life here. That way lay madness.

Fortunately, the door creaked open a moment later. A towering man stood in front of us, gaunt and skeletal. Ophelia's butler was some kind of a wraith, but he never shared the details. Like demons, there were many types. It wasn't my business to ask, however.

"Is Ophelia home?" I asked, getting right down to it. I'd once tried making small talk with him, but he'd had no interest.

He gave one curt nod, and I felt my shoulders loosen. As I stepped over the threshold into her beautifully decorated home, I relaxed even further. Nothing bad had ever happened to me here, and it was going to stay that way. We would get in and get out and be home in New Orleans within the hour.

Talan followed me into the foyer, his gaze alert on our surroundings. Ophelia's house was as safe and boring as it looked. The traditional decor was more suited to a human home, but she liked it that way. The only magic in the entire place came from her and the protections on the perimeter of the house. It was a vault of safety, which was one of the main reasons I liked her so much.

"This way." The butler's voice rumbled low as he gestured for us to follow him down the hall. He led us to a sitting room, one that I had waited in many times before.

I took a seat on the couch and nodded for Talan to do the same. He sat next to me, and the small size of the sofa meant that I could almost feel the heat of him blistering my side.

The butler left, shutting the door behind him. Talan leaned close and murmured, "You're sure this is the woman?"

"I know it's not your normal witch's house, but, I'm sure."

"Will she make us wait long?"

"Generally not."

Two minutes later, the door creaked open, and the scent of sandalwood wafted into the room. A short woman followed it, her curvy figure wrapped in a tailored suit that looked like it was from the 1950s. It made her look like any other New York socialite. Little did the world know that she was far from normal, no matter how she dressed when she went to Whole Foods for her weekly shopping.

She approached with a graceful stride, almost

floating on the air. Her perfectly painted lips curved into a catlike smile, and she nearly purred at the sight of Talan. "Well, hello there."

I didn't bother saying anything. She clearly had eyes only for Talan, and since I wanted her help, I was happy to let her focus on the object of her desire. Anyway, she had no idea that I had left town. As far she was concerned, I still lived here. It wasn't a big deal that I was back.

She propped her hip on the side table that sat next to the fireplace and smiled at Talan. "What brings such a handsome demon to my door?"

He gave her an easy smile. "We need some help with a spell."

Her gaze moved to me for the first time, and her lips twisted in a frown. "It's dangerous for you to be here."

The iron fist tightened around my heart once more. "You know?"

She nodded. "He sent one of his goons to ask if I knew where you went."

I felt Talan's interest pique. I shook my head subtly, hoping she would get the message. I didn't want to talk about this around him.

"We have a big problem," I said. "We're only here for a little while, and we were hoping you could help." I leaned forward. "We need a spell that will reveal hidden magic that has been used in a specific spot. We'll pay anything." Talan would pay anything. *I* had nothing to pay with. She knew that because I usually traded favors for the magic she gave me.

She made a low noise in her throat and crossed her arms, tapping her fingers rhythmically against her biceps. "What's at stake?"

"The lives of my people." Talan's voice had gone low with the severity of the situation. "I'm Talan, the demon lord of New Orleans. The portal that keeps my people on this plane is malfunctioning due to a spell. Someone is trying to destabilize what I built, and as a result, my people are disappearing."

"You think you know who's behind it?" she asked. "You're just looking for proof?"

Talan nodded. "Precisely."

She hummed again. "You'd better be careful with that. Assumptions never lead to anything good."

"True enough." Talan stood and approached her, stopping far enough away that his great size wasn't a threat. "You're right, and we'll keep an open mind. I wouldn't want to be swayed by my own biases."

Ophelia leaned far to the right, so that she could see around Talan's shoulders, and met my gaze. Her eyebrows lifted. "I like this one. Men are usually so..." She waved a hand. "You know what I mean. Not very open-minded."

"Definitely not the men we normally work with," I said.

"All right. For old time's sake, I'll help you. But you

can never come back here again. He'll be angry if he finds out you contacted me, and I didn't tell him."

"I understand, and I'm sorry if we put you at risk."

She waved her hand. "I'll be fine. Now let me get what you need. Stay here."

She left the room, and Talan turned to look at me. I could feel the interest nearly bubbling out of him. "What has she been talking about?"

"None of your business." I rose and walked to the window to look outside.

Immediately, my gaze landed on a man across the street. He wore dark, nondescript clothing, and his expression was flat. Yet, from the way he stared hard at Ophelia's place, it was obvious who he was—one of my old boss's goons.

Dammit. I had definitely triggered a spell when I'd returned to town, and it had taken no time to send this guy over here. He wouldn't be able to get into Ophelia's place, but I would have to be smart when we left.

I felt Talan's presence at my back before he spoke. "Who's that?"

"Just a guy, I guess."

"You and I both know that's not true.".

Dammit again. Talan was too smart for this, but I didn't want him to know anything about my past. If he asked too many questions, he would find out what I was.

"Let's just say it's my business." I slipped away from him before I became lulled by the sense of security that his proximity brought. If life had taught me anything, it was that I could only count on myself. I needed to stay on my toes.

Fortunately, Ophelia returned a moment later, carrying a small glass sphere in her hands. Within the orb, a smoky white haze swirled. She held it out to Talan, who took it. Her gaze went to the window, narrowing. "I see we already have guests. You should head out the back."

"Will you be okay?" I asked.

She laughed. "Of course, I will be. I'll let him in to look around, and by the time he leaves, he'll forget he was ever here."

I smiled, grateful to know that she could take care of herself. The last thing I wanted was to arrive in town and screw her over.

"Thank you," I said. "I appreciate it."

"Good. Now go." She waved us out, then turned and went to the front door to welcome the man in.

Her butler led us through the house to the back alley. There might be someone waiting out there as well, but it was less likely. Anyway, I wasn't about to ask her for more help than she'd already given.

"You have to tell me what's going on," Talan said.

"I really don't."

We slipped out into the alley, which was empty as far as I could tell. The portal wasn't far away, but we'd have to get there without being seen.

"Come on, this way." I turned left, heading toward the end of the alley. It looked like a dead end, with a brick wall that rose twelve feet in front of us.

"Are you sure about this? It doesn't look like there's a way out," Talan said.

"I'm sure." I stopped in front of the brick wall and reached up, sinking my fingertips into two divots in the wall that had been created by missing bricks. A few feet from the ground, there was another one for my right foot. I slipped my toes in and began to climb, using the divots that weren't apparent to the eyes, but that I knew were there.

When I reached the top, I swung my leg over and dropped down onto the other side. The smell of baked cheese and bread filled the air in the tiny courtyard behind the pizza place. If we had more time, I would've grabbed a slice. It had been my favorite when I'd lived here.

Talan dropped down beside me. He gave the little courtyard a considering look. "While you're telling me about the guys stalking you, I'd also like to know why you're so familiar with escape routes around New York."

"You'll be waiting a long time." I hurried into the little pizza parlor and waved to the guys behind the counter. They barely acknowledged me, not looking up from their work. It was the perfect reaction as far as I was concerned. I led Talan through the restaurant and onto a side street. We just had to cross the main road to get to the alley with the portal, and we'd be good.

Of course, we weren't so lucky.

As we were hurrying across the road, I caught sight of two men about thirty yards away.

"Shit." I grabbed Talan's hand and pulled him into a run. We wouldn't make it all the way to the alley, but there was a recessed doorway that would provide some cover.

We threw ourselves into it, and Talan forced me into the corner, making a shield of his own body.

"Hey." I tried to shove him out of the way, but he didn't move. Stubborn man.

Instead, he leaned back to look out at the street. He cursed low in his throat, then ducked back, curling his body protectively over mine. A moment later, a sonic boom hit him.

He jerked as if he'd been shot, but anyone who was familiar with sonic booms knew that they were far worse than a measly bullet. And yet, Talan didn't go to his knees like any normal man. Instead, he stayed standing, still shielding me.

"They're fast," he grunted.

Shit. Now that he'd been hit with a sonic boom, I knew who was after us. I hadn't recognized them out in the street, but if I had, I might not have chosen to take cover in the doorway.

"This is a human neighborhood. We should try not to use any obvious magic," I said.

He nodded curtly, then turned around to face the street. Licks of flame had begun to curl around his arms, thin tendrils of fire that wouldn't be visible from far away. I could feel their heat, but it wasn't painful. The fire twisted from his arms to his torso and then down his legs. It fed into the ground, and I watched, fascinated, as it streaked across the road in a thin line.

I peered around Talan's shoulder and spotted the two men approaching us from across the street. The mage who could throw sonic booms had his hands raised, as if he were about to deliver another one.

Before he could, the flame stopped directly beneath him and his partner. They jerked to a halt, their faces twisting in pain. I couldn't see what was happening to them, but whatever it was, it was bad. Real bad.

"They're burning from the inside," Talan said as he grabbed my hand. "Let's go."

I'd never seen such horrific—or powerful—magic before, and it left me slightly stunned. I let him drag me out of the alley, adrenaline and the movement pulling me back into the moment.

I scouted the street as we ran toward the alley with the portal, looking for more attackers. It was a quiet road at this time of day, and I saw no one—until we entered the alley.

Three of them appeared from the shadows, and I

recognized them immediately as some of my old boss's most powerful assassins. Gordon, with the electricity sparking around his skinny limbs. Malachai, who walked upon clouds of black smoke that would choke a person as it fed them their most awful nightmares. And Ferris, who had strength and speed that made him even more dangerous than me.

They stood between us and the portal, a deadly wall.

"Stay back," Talan said to me.

"Ha."

He charged toward the men, and I followed. Immediately, he clashed with Gordon and Malachai. They were the most obviously dangerous, but I wouldn't choose to fight any of them.

Unfortunately, that choice wasn't mine.

Flame burst to life around Talan, but it was the last I saw of their fight. Ferris was headed straight for me. I needed to stay out of his grip if I wanted any chance at all. I might be able to kill with a touch, but he knew that and was fast enough not to give me a chance. He was also wearing head-to-toe black leather with only his face showing. I couldn't even see the skin of his hands or neck. Since I needed to make contact with his skin, that left me with almost no space to work with if I wanted to use my deadly power against him.

I plunged my hand into my pocket. Withdrawing a potion bomb, I hurled it at him, but he batted it aside like a cat with a toy. It crashed against the wall, the deadly green liquid splattering the bricks.

Damn it.

I tried again, throwing another bomb. He knocked that one aside, too, advancing on me with determined strides. A sick kind of pleasure twisted his features, and cold fear gripped my insides.

As a last resort, I drew my karambit, swiping it out toward him. I landed a blow to his chest that sank deep. Blood welled, staining his shirt, but he kept coming. I sliced at him again, landing another blow, but it wasn't enough.

He had his hand around my throat in an instant and slammed me against the brick wall so hard that I felt my ribs crack. Pain exploded inside me, and he began to tighten his grip.

My air supply cut off immediately, but that wasn't the worst of it. I could feel him crushing my windpipe, the pain so great that I nearly blacked out.

Evil glee lit his eyes. Ferris had never liked me—we were too evenly matched. I'd threatened his spot on the top rung of the ladder, even though I had no interest in being there. He was delighted to have the opportunity to kill me.

I wouldn't give him the chance. At least, not without killing him first. I was already dead—I could feel it from the way my throat was ruined. But I had enough strength left to take him with me.

Anger gave me extra fuel as I plunged my blade into his gut. Surprise flashed in his eyes—he hadn't expected me to be able to do that, considering the sorry state I was in.

I took advantage of his distraction and grabbed his wrist with a viselike grip. There was the tiniest gap between his glove and jacket, and I forced my hand inside until my flesh met his. I didn't hesitate as I fed my deadly magic into him.

The fear that I would normally feel at discovery was gone. I was nothing but desperation now, even though I knew I'd never come back from these wounds. My vision was already going dark from lack of air.

But my magic worked, and Ferris dropped like a stone. Without his hand supporting me, I collapsed to the ground next to him. The last thing I saw was Talan, standing over the bodies of the other two men, staring at me with a stricken expression.

Then everything went dark.

10

Talan

Stunned, I watched Cora collapse to the ground. I'd taken out the two most obvious threats, but it seemed I'd been mistaken about who was the most dangerous.

He lay dead at her feet, but she didn't look much better.

Cold terror streaked through me. Running to her, I gathered her into my arms. She was limp, her eyelids fluttering, and the damage to her throat was readily apparent.

She couldn't breathe. I had minutes before she died —maybe less.

I turned and sprinted for the portal, driven by a fear unlike any I'd ever felt. The portal sucked us through and spun us through space. I clutched her to me, stumbling out into my home and roaring for the healer.

Liora appeared as I strode from the room.

"What happened?" she asked.

"Send the healer to my room. *Now.*"

Her gaze moved to Cora's slack form, and her eyes widened. She spun on her heel and ran.

I reached my chambers in record time and laid her gently on the bed. Her face was pale as she struggled to breathe. Every labored breath appeared to be intensely painful, and I couldn't tell if she was actually getting any air into her lungs.

The healer raced into the room a moment later, panting and wild-eyed. Her gray curls were wrapped in a towel, and the bathrobe that she wore flapped around her legs as she hurried over to the bed.

"What are we dealing with?" she demanded, her tone as commanding as ever. Catriona was the best healer in the southeast, and part of that came from her ability to cut to the heart of a situation.

"Crushed throat, at the minimum. She's been without air for at least a minute. Possibly two."

She nodded, her gaze determined, and knelt by the bed so that she was closer to Cora. "Give me space."

I stepped back, but the movement was difficult. Getting even a few feet away from Cora made something roar to life inside me. It was the mate bond—I knew it had to be—but it was more than that.

I would be devastated if I lost her. Not just as a result of the bond, but because I cared for her. I hardly knew her, and yet, I knew enough that she had become immensely important to me. I didn't want to imagine a life without her powerful presence. Her intelligence, wit, humor, and strength were bright points in my bleak existence.

I'd been avoiding her because she distracted me from my duties to my people, but now that she lay dying, I realized what a mistake I'd made.

I watched, breath held, as Catriona hovered her hand over Cora's throat. Her magic swelled on the air, smelling of herbs and spice.

When Cora finally sucked in a ragged breath, the rush of adrenaline leaving my body made me weak. A pained sigh escaped me, surprising me. I'd had no idea that I was holding my breath until Cora could take one of her own, but apparently, I had been. Worry had hijacked my brain, further proof that I shouldn't be involved with her because it made me lose control of myself.

And yet, I couldn't fight the desire to be close to her. As Catriona rose, I moved forward, drawn to Cora like a planet drawn to its sun.

She blinked up at me, dazed.

"She'll be fine," Catriona said softly. "Broken ribs and a crushed windpipe, but they're repaired now."

Catriona was worth every penny I paid her. "Thank you."

She disappeared from my side, and I sat at the edge of the bed, my fingertips itching to touch Cora. I wanted to speak but had no idea what to say. The fear of losing her still froze my tongue.

How the hell had she gotten away from that bastard, though? One moment she was being strangled, the next, her attacker had collapsed. And yet, there was no sign of a wound.

That had to have something to do with her unexplained magic.

"I didn't expect to survive that," Cora said, distracting me from my thoughts. I was relieved to hear that her voice was surprisingly strong. It shook with the faintest edge of fear, though. "I thought I was going to die."

Cora

I stared up at Talan, my mind spinning with everything that had just happened.

I'd almost died.

I would have died, except for the swiftness of Talan's

actions. But it was the way Talan looked at me that really shook me.

He was looking at me like he cared. Like, *really* cared. The tenderness and fear in his eyes were a strange combination. It reached inside my chest and squeezed. Combined with the memory of running out of air and knowing I would die, it was too much.

A wave of emotion crashed over me, so strong that I couldn't stop it. I lunged toward Talan and wrapped my arms around his neck, hugging him tight.

A low noise escaped him, and he pulled me into his arms, cradling me against him. The feeling of being protected washed over me, followed by a wave of heat. It was impossible to ignore how good he felt. Strong and warm.

And he smelled divine, like spice and fire and *him.* There was just *something* about his scent—drawing it into my lungs made my heart light up.

The fear of dying morphed quickly into an intense desire to feel alive. I wanted to press every inch of my body to Talan's, to forget the fear in a wash of pleasure.

When I looked up and met his gaze, I saw heat in his eyes that reflected what I felt in my core.

"Talan," I whispered, raising my hand to his cheek.

He didn't pull back. The heat in his gaze became an inferno, and it was enough to push me over the edge. I leaned up and kissed him, pressing my lips to his.

A low groan escaped him, and his hand plunged into my hair at the back of my head, cupping me to him as his mouth devoured mine. I wrapped my arms tighter around his neck and clung to him, never wanting to let go.

He laid me back on the bed and kissed me like he would die if he couldn't. He made me feel like the center of his world, and I liked it. A lot.

When he dragged his lips down my neck, I arched into him, breathing his name on a sigh.

He paused briefly, as if waiting for me to object, but he'd be waiting forever for that. When I ran my hands down his shoulders and to his sides, he kept going, kissing down to my stomach.

His fingertips brushed the sliver of skin over the waistband of my jeans, and I gasped. When his mouth followed the path, I arched into his kisses. My head spun from the pleasure, and when I felt his fingers at the button of my jeans, I looked down.

His gaze burned up at me. "May I?"

The air rushed out of my lungs, and I nodded. The next moments passed in a haze of pleasure. He deftly undid the fastenings of my jeans, and they were around my ankles a moment later.

He buried his face against my panties, and I arched into him. The low groan that escaped him vibrated against me, and I shivered. When he removed the thin cotton and pressed his mouth to my flesh, I gasped.

He gripped my hips and held me like a man

possessed, as if he couldn't get enough of me. The feel of his mouth made my head spin, the pleasure building to a fever pitch, a train that was about to plow into me.

When it did, I cried out and clutched his head, my fingers sunk into his soft hair.

He pulled away, and I looked up at him, a haze of pleasure surrounding me. I gestured for him to come toward me—I wanted to kiss him like he'd kissed me—but he shook his head.

I blinked, stunned. "What?"

He dragged a hand through his hair, his mouth swollen, and pupils dilated. The expression on his face was nothing short of tortured. "We should stop."

"Stop?" After I'd just gotten off and he still had an impressive length pressing against the front of his jeans?

"It was a mistake," he said, his voice flat.

Hurt streaked through me, then guilt. *Fiona.* She relied on me, but here I was, trying to convince the demon lord to get in bed with me. An offer that he'd *refused.* While I wasn't wearing pants.

Just...wow.

"Of course." I scrambled upright, dressing while he turned around.

"I'll meet you in the front hall," he said. "We'll get Calex here while we deploy the spell."

"Good idea." I didn't look at him, but I could hear him. He was near the door.

He left without another word, and I flopped back on

the bed. What the hell had I just done? I scrubbed my hands over my face and decided to forget it. What had just happened had been a moment of insanity brought on by nearly dying.

And Talan was right—it was a bad idea to get involved. He'd chosen a terrible time and way to tell me, because, hell, that kind of rejection was hard on a girl's self-esteem. But it was the best way forward. I needed to focus on helping Fiona and finding out what was going wrong in New Orleans.

I liked the fact that we were including enforcement. Not only did I not want to be alone with Talan right now, but his willingness to include enforcement made it even less likely he was involved with the disappearances. Not that I thought he would do anything to put his people at risk—I knew enough about him to be sure of that.

I finished dressing and tried to force aside my embarrassment as I strode down to the main hall. I found Talan standing in the middle of the room, so I began to walk the perimeter. I didn't want to stand still long enough to talk about what had just happened between us. And what if he'd seen how I'd killed Ferris? Would he ask me about it?

It was better to stay on the move. I stopped in front of a painting. A beautiful woman in a scarlet silk dress, a demon with tiny horns and brilliant blue eyes was posed in front of a black and red hellscape.

"Who is this? A girlfriend?" As soon as the words left my mouth, I wanted to die. What the hell was I thinking? *This* was why I didn't have friends.

"My mother."

Perfect. Even better. "Right, that makes more sense. How is she doing?"

He hesitated, then spoke. "I haven't seen her since I was 14."

"You should visit more often."

"She's dead."

Wow, I was on fire here. Could I have put my foot any deeper in my mouth? I shot him a look over my shoulder, hoping to convey how sorry I was but unable to turn and make any kind of true connection. "I'm sorry. That sucks."

"It is what it is." But there were shadows in his eyes that made me think it still hurt him. "I'm not even sure how good that likeness is. I had it painted from my memory."

"She was beautiful."

Talan's phone buzzed, and he removed it to read a text. I was grateful for the distraction. Somehow, I'd managed to go from sex straight into a discussion of dead mothers. I was batting a thousand, digging us deeper into awkwardness.

A moment later, Talan said, "Calex is here."

He opened the main door, leaning against the door jamb while he waited for our acquaintance. A few minutes later, Calex made his way up the stairs and into the foyer.

He smiled when he saw us. "You got the spell?" he asked.

"We did," Talan said. "We're going to go deploy it now. Thought you might want to be there."

"Damned right I do," Calex said. "A day listening to the horrific stories of missing family members has me itching to solve this one fast."

"Follow me." Talan turned and left the foyer, heading down the wide hallway toward the back of the house. Calex and I followed, and I tried to put the last hour from my mind.

As we neared the back of the house, I felt the pulse of dark magic. We descended slowly, and I breathed shallowly, not wanting to draw any of it into my lungs.

He led us down the rest of the stairs and into an empty room. On the far side, a glowing silver portal pulsed with power. My skin chilled, and I stopped dead in my tracks, driven by instinct. Talan shot me a look, understanding in his eyes. Even under the best of circumstances, I would be wary of approaching the portal to a demon underworld. Considering that this portal tended to suck unwilling victims inside...

Yeah, I'd be staying back here.

"I'll deploy the spell," Talan said. He pulled the small round vial from his pocket and uncorked it, walking up to the portal to pour the silver liquid to the ground in front of it. As the liquid smoked, a new type of magic began to vibrate on the air. It grew in strength, electricity sparking in bright bursts.

As we watched, silvery wisps of smoke rose from the puddle at the base of the portal to form letters.

"What are those?" Calex murmured.

I squinted at them. They weren't letters at all.

They were runes. They floated through the air, symbols of great power that I couldn't decipher. Next to me, Calex muttered something unintelligible, frustration echoing in his tone.

As the symbols faded away, Talan turned to look at us. "What the hell were the damned fae doing down here?"

"The fae?" I asked. "I thought it was Rathbine, from your underworld."

"I thought it was. But this isn't his type of magic. This is distinctly fae."

I frowned. "I thought they couldn't come to the city very often?"

"Under most circumstances, they are unable to," Calex said. "They need to be close to their realm, or they wither without its magic."

I've never heard of that happening to fae before, but these fae were quite far from their homeland, and perhaps that was part of it.

"What could they want with your portal, then?" I asked.

"Perhaps they want a foothold in the city," Talan said. "This portal allows my people, who shouldn't be able to stay on Earth, to remain here. The fae suffer from a similar type of restriction."

"So, you think they might be planning to manipulate the portal to give themselves access to New Orleans?" Calex asked.

"It makes as much sense as anything." A deep frown creased Talan's face. "We need to find out what the hell is going on."

"I'm heading out," Calex said. "I have some things I want to check on. Maybe a new lead."

Before we could ask him more, he was gone, his footsteps echoing on the stairs.

"I need to get out of here, too." I turned to walk up the stairs, looking back at Talan. I wanted to talk to him, just the hell away from the portal. "Are you coming?"

He gazed at the portal, which continued to pulse with power. The smoke from the runes was already wafting away. There was nothing left to see down there.

He turned back to me. "I am."

I led the way up the stairs, anxiety vibrating through me. I didn't like this new development. The fae were powerful. I'd left the party with the knowledge of their strength.

When I reached the top floor, I turned and headed back to the foyer. Halfway to my destination, I spotted a small library on the right. It was empty, and I slipped inside. Talan followed me, a questioning expression creasing his brow.

"Why were you so cozy with the fae queen at the party?" I asked.

He frowned. "I would hardly say I was cozy."

"I don't know. You looked pretty friendly with her. And now we've learned that fae magic is being used to manipulate your portal."

"And you think I helped them?"

"Who better than the owner of this house to help a stranger sneak around?" I wasn't sure I believed that, but I couldn't help but ask. And I was still so unsettled after what had just happened between us that my judgement might be shaky.

"The queen invited me to the party. I hadn't seen her in years. We don't socialize, and there's no mutual business between us the way there is with the other faction leaders. I was curious what she wanted from me."

"And? What did she want?"

"She wanted to shove us together."

I felt my jaw slacken. "What?"

"She knows we're mates. She also suspected that I would resist the bond. So she…"

So she wanted to put us together. "Why, though?"

"Honestly, I have no idea. I'd like to say it's because she was bored, but I don't think that's it. I think there was more to it. Maybe she wanted me out of the house so she could do something to the portal."

"We need to get back onto her turf and poke around, then."

Talan nodded. "Agreed. One problem though—we won't be able to sneak in. Their wards are too powerful"

"Then we need an invitation." I arched a brow. "And I think I know just the guy to get us one."

"I'm going to assume you are not talking about Calex."

"You would be right. Get to it, Demon Lord. We need to get into the fae realm."

11

Cora

When the phone rang a few hours later, I grabbed it immediately. I swiped to accept the call and raised the phone to my ear. "Yes?"

"I've got us an invitation for tonight," Talan said.

"Excellent. What kind of invitation?"

"That's the part you might not love. It's a weekend house party, and we're invited to the entire thing."

"That's great! We'll have plenty of time to look around."

"True. But we will have to pretend to be a couple for the amount of time we're there. A weekend is a long time."

Oh, shit.

After what had just happened in his bedroom, pretending to be a couple was going to be tough. The opportunity for awkwardness was off the charts. And if we couldn't convince the fake queen we were the real deal, she could turn on us while we were alone on her turf.

That said, we didn't have many options.

"Do you think she'll believe we're a couple?" I asked.

"Maybe. Traditionally, the mate bond is strong and hard to fight." I heard the slightest awkward pause on the line before he said, "Not that it's a problem for us, of course."

Ouch. "Right. Of course." I hoped he couldn't hear how much that had hurt.

"I told her we wanted to have dinner with her to thank her for bringing us together," he said. "But she could still be suspicious. We'll have to be careful."

"So we could be walking into a trap."

"There's already a trap in my basement," he said, his tone tight. "Honestly, I'll feel safer on their turf."

I chuckled, but it was the dark kind of laughter that came when someone was joking about something bad. "Good point. What time do we leave? And what kind of clothing do I need for this thing?"

"We'll leave at 6:30. You'll need attire for dinner parties and casual."

"All right. I can do that." Thanks to Mia.

After I hung up with Talan, I went over to Mia's

place. Fiona braved the trip with me, reasoning that she was close enough to the house that if the portal went off again, she would still benefit from its proximity.

Mia let us into the café and put a little CLOSED FOR 10 MINUTES sign on the door. She then led us upstairs and helped me put together the perfect wardrobe. Fiona sat in the corner, quietly observing. Worry tightened her features, and the sight of it fueled my determination to find out what was going on with the fae queen.

Once the wardrobe was packed away in one of Mia's spare suitcases, she looked me up and down. "You need to shower before you go."

"Rude." I grinned. "But you're not wrong. I'll go do that. Good luck with the café the rest of the night. And thanks again."

"Anytime." She gave me a quick hug and stepped back. "Since you're going onto fae territory with the demon lord and you won't have any backup, you should ask Rei what she might have to help you." She grimaced. "Like a transport charm to get you out of there if things get dicey."

"That's a good idea. I have a few things left from my old life, but no transport charms." My stash of potion bombs was running perilously low too, and I didn't have a truth potion. That would be invaluable if we were trying to get information out of the fae queen.

"Then get out of here and give her a call," Mia said.

I saluted her, then turned to look at Fiona, who had

been uncharacteristically quiet this entire time. "You ready go?"

"Yeah, definitely." She turned and drifted toward the door.

"I worry about her," Mia whispered so that Fiona couldn't hear. "I think this is making it more obvious to her that she's dead, and she could disappear from this plane at any time."

"I know. I feel like hell that my mother was the one to kill her. I owe it to her to find a way to keep her here."

"You'll do it."

I gave her a smile of gratitude and turned to leave. I dropped Fiona off at home, then spent the next two hours helping Rei make the potions for tonight. She already had a transport charm in stock, which was a good thing because they usually took a few days to make. We also put together some potion bombs and acid bombs, along with an all-important truth potion. Talan might bring one, but I wanted to be prepared myself. Rei's calico cat watched us with wise eyes as we mixed the ingredients and poured them into the little glass vials. After I corked one, I smiled at her. "Thanks for letting me help with this. I've never made these before."

"No problem. I like having the help. And the company." A concerned expression crossed her face. "Are you sure about this? No one ever goes onto fae land except during the big bacchanal."

"Why not?"

"We're scared, silly." She shrugged. "That's why we're all so excited by the bacchanal. Not just because it's a great party, but because we can enter forbidden territory but be safe."

"I'll be careful. But it's the only way forward as far as we can tell."

"I think you're right. At the very least, you have to figure out how the fae magic got into the demon lord's basement."

"Could someone else have bought the magic from the queen? Like, maybe the fae aren't involved, beyond selling the magic?"

"Not likely, though it's possible. But she's notoriously proud. She'd have to have a damned good reason to sell it, and I can't imagine what that is."

"So, she's probably involved with this." I grimaced. That made it more dangerous to go onto her turf. But I wanted my answers, and I had to save Fiona. "All right then, I'm out of here. Thanks for everything."

"Anytime."

I went home and cleaned up. As I left, Fiona waited in the kitchen, sitting in her favorite spot on the counter next to Balthazar and his toaster. She swung her legs and looked at me, worry creasing her brow.

I heaved my overnight bag onto my shoulder and met her gaze. "It's going to be fine. I promise."

"I don't like the idea of you going into danger for me."

"You don't have to like it. It's happening."

"But—"

I heard the sound of a car approaching and interrupted her. "He's here. Gotta go. Stay safe."

I left before she could say anything else. We'd agreed it would be safer for her to stay here, since this was where she felt strongest and most grounded to reality. She was also wearing the bracelet that kept her bound to me, so that would help protect her from the portal's pull.

I slipped out of the bookshop and down the short flight of stairs to the street. The car idled in the road, waiting. The driver stayed behind the wheel, and Talan got out to open the door for me. He took my bag and put it in the trunk.

"Thanks." I slipped into the car, and he followed.

Once again, I was surrounded by the incredible wealth that was so common in Talan's life. I'd never been in a luxury car until I'd come to New Orleans and met him. Not to mention his house.

Mostly, it made me feel like I didn't fit in.

Which I didn't, and it was good to remember that. I was building a life on the quirky side of town with my friends. I shouldn't be getting used to the life of the demon lord.

Anyway, it was better to focus on how I didn't fit into

his life than the awkwardness between us after the event in his bedroom.

"There will be six other couples there," Talan said.

"All fae?"

"No. Witches, a vampire, shifters. It's a mixed group. The queen likes inviting outsiders to parties."

"It sounds like she's getting bored in her perfect, protected little world."

"She probably is. She was once a warrior. She had to be to create her realm. But they've had peace and prosperity for so long that she could be looking for a challenge."

"That can't be good." It made me think of house cats with sharp teeth and deadly claws. They watched the birds out the window, desperate to murder—out of boredom and instinct. The fae queen had both.

"So, what's our cover story?" I asked.

"We need to keep it simple. Something we can both remember easily. It hasn't been long since the party, and the queen has an ego. She'll enjoy knowing she set us up. I'll say that her words were the push I needed."

"Do you think she'll buy it?"

He shrugged. "I'm not sure she even buys our reason for wanting to come. But we needed an in, and we've got it."

"Good point. And the story works for me. I'll say we've been inseparable since then, thanks to the mate bond." I hated that the story didn't sound so far-fetched.

I was fighting the connection with him, but it still lit the air up with electricity whenever I was near him.

"We're almost there." He reached into his pocket and pulled out a small box, then handed it to me. "Here, put this on."

I took the box, which was covered in the softest velvet I'd ever touched. I flipped it open to reveal a ruby pendant that blazed with fire. I felt the air rush from my lungs. I didn't know anything about jewelry, but I knew this was valuable. It was also vaguely familiar. "What's this?"

"It was my mother's. The queen is traditional in some ways. The fact that you wear my mother's ruby will go far to convince her of our story."

That's where I'd seen the jewel. "I'll take good care of it."

"Thank you. It's all I have left of her. Besides the memories, though those are few and far between"

My heart hurt for him, and I wished I knew what to say. How could we have shared such an intimate moment earlier today, but I was still unable to offer words of comfort?

My early life had broken me.

Fortunately, the car slowed, distracting me from my dire thoughts. I looked out the window. We were approaching the entry to the fae court. Magic swelled on the air, pressing in on me, and I drew in a deep breath.

Let the games begin.

12

Cora

The car rolled to a stop in front of the massive silver gate. Through the car window, I could see that it had been decorated with fresh flowers twisted around the ornate silver bars. The magic that pulsed around it seemed to glow with a silver light and beckoned me forth.

"Why wasn't the gate like this during the party?" I asked.

It had just been a normal gate. Beautiful and made of delicate silver, but it hadn't pulsed with such incredible magic.

"For the party, they lower the protections on their realm to let so many people in. This is how it normally looks—if you've been invited, at least. Otherwise, it's invisible."

The car passed through the gate, and the feeling was even more intense than the first time. The incredible pressure made every cell in my body tighten. When it passed, I slumped against the seat.

The skin on the back of my neck tightened as we rolled down the drive, and I realized how damned dangerous this was.

"I have a transport charm if we need to get out of here quickly," I said.

"So do I," he said. "Don't hesitate to use yours if you need to. Leave me behind, I can take care of myself."

That was the truth.

The car stopped, and Talan climbed out. I got out before he could open my door and joined him on his side of the car.

He held out his arm for me, and I looked at it, my brow raised.

He didn't lower it. "We are supposed to be a couple, remember?"

Of course. It was going to involve touching each other. I gave him a smile and reached for his arm, trying to shove away the memories of earlier. The steel of his muscles was enough to send a shiver through my body. I hated the effect he had on me, but it was impossible to deny.

"The driver will bring our bags." Talan started toward the gate, and I matched my steps to his.

The woods looked far different than they had during the party. Without the musicians, partiers, and tables full of delicacies, it looked quiet and serene. A pathway had been built through the trees. Fashioned of beautiful golden wood, it formed a walkway about a foot above the ground. Fairy lights sparkled all around it, lighting the way through the Bayou.

We started down the path, walking farther than I had the first night. Soon, we were on land that I hadn't seen before. "Are we almost there?"

"The palace is up ahead."

"Palace?"

"Have you ever known the fae to live in anything less than an extraordinary castle?"

"Good point. I just figured being in the Bayou..."

"Nothing will stop them." He nodded toward the view ahead, and I looked in the direction he pointed.

"Wow." I stared at the gorgeous, delicate structure that had been built of golden wood and pale, smooth stone. It was a legitimate castle, surrounded by massive oak trees draped in Spanish moss. Tall towers rose above the trees, reaching toward the starlit sky. Many of them had massive windows, and some even lacked glass in the panes, giving it an open-air feel. Pale silver pennants flew from the tops of each tower, and spiral staircases wound their way around the outsides of the structures. Delicate arched bridges connected the towers, and the entire place had the feel of an aerial treehouse built among the branches.

"This place is incredible," I said. "No wonder they don't let people back here. No one would ever want to leave."

"True, but the beauty hides great danger." His arm tightened to pull me closer to his side, a protective gesture that I couldn't help but like.

"Come." We walked the rest of the way in silence, ascending the wide set of stairs that led to the front doors. The two massive wooden doors had been carved with an ornate forest scene. I could spend hours looking at it, but the doors swung open as soon as we stopped in front of it.

A tall, slender man with golden hair and pale blue eyes smiled politely at us. He wore a sky-blue uniform festooned with silver buttons that glinted in the light as he bowed low. "Welcome. The queen is expecting you."

He stepped back to allow us to enter, and we crossed the threshold into a large, airy atrium. The ceiling above was clear glass that reflected the candlelight below. There were no electric lights that I could see—just glimmering ivory tapers. Hundreds of them. Maybe thousands. And yet, no dripping wax. As if the fae would ever allow wax to sully their beautiful home.

The man led us down a long exterior pathway. Overhead, an arched roof protected us from the sky, but there were no windows. Warm night air swirled around me as we made our way to the next tower. It was lovely now, but what about on a summer day?

I leaned close to Talan and whispered, "What do they do when it's sweltering or pouring?"

"Magic," he whispered back. "Climate controlling this place is a huge power suck. Honestly, I have no idea exactly how they manage it."

"Seems like it shouldn't be possible."

He shrugged, and I supposed that was one thing about the magical world—anything was possible. You just had to find a way to make it happen.

When we reached the next tower, the doors swung open to welcome us. When we stepped through, the sounds of the party rushed over me. The cocktail party was already underway. The faintest hint of danger lingered in the air, along with the more obvious note of revelry. People were laughing and talking, all dressed to impress.

At least Mia had properly outfitted me once again. My short black dress fit in perfectly, and I hoped nobody would give me a second glance. It would make snooping much easier.

"This way." Talan led me toward a table where a bartender was mixing the most beautiful cocktails I'd ever seen. They were pale shades of pink, purple, and blue, and many of them glittered or smoked. I kept my gaze on the crowd around us as Talan ordered. There were a dozen people here, but not the queen. I spotted two fae couples, immediately obvious from their ethereal beauty and pointed ears. Behind them stood a vampire couple, and along the wall were four that were likely shifters.

I turned back to Talan. "Do you know these people?"

"I've met all of them at one time or another, though we don't socialize." He handed me a glittering golden concoction. I took a sip, entranced by the taste of champagne and fruit. I've never had anything like it, and if I weren't careful, I could drink the lot.

"You don't socialize with many people though, do you?" I asked.

"You've got me there." He smiled at me, clearly trying to look like we were having a regular conversation. "Shall we mingle and make sure that everybody thinks we're normal?"

I nodded. It was vital that nobody suspected us of snooping. I linked my arm through his and grinned up at him. "Lead the way."

Talan sipped the dark amber liquid in his glass and strolled toward the nearest couple.

The dark-haired man and pale woman were obviously vampires. Their smiles revealed pointed fangs, and the magic that wafted off them smelled faintly of blood.

"Marcus and Aurelia," Talan said. "It's been such a long time. I don't think you've met my mate yet?"

He looped his arm around my shoulders and squeezed me tight to his side.

An almost overwhelming sense of belonging washed through me. Suddenly, I desperately wanted to be part of a pair like this. A pair with him. I'd been alone so long that the idea of sharing my life with someone was tantalizing.

And totally terrifying.

I held out my hand. "I'm Cora."

Marcus shook my hand, and then Aurelia. We chatted for a little while, and though they seemed nice enough, there was something dark in their gazes. A latent threat, like a snake coiled tight, waiting to strike.

When the conversation was over, I was grateful to move on to another pair. The shifters that we met— Rowan and Sam—were just as creepy as the vampires, but in their own way. I shouldn't be surprised that the queen was friends with the most dangerous supernaturals in New Orleans.

Partway through the conversation, I excused myself to find the restroom. More than anything, I just wanted a quiet moment to myself.

One of the circulating waiters directed me toward an ornate, multi-person bathroom. There was a long vanity punctuated by three ivory sinks. Above the sinks sat an enormous gilt mirror.

I washed my hands but resisted splashing water on

my face, even though I desperately wanted to. I didn't need to look like a drowned rat when I left, however.

I turned to go, nearly bumping into another woman as she entered the bathroom. Her brilliant red curls were piled on the top of her head, and her pointed ears marked her as one of the fae. I gave her a polite smile and tried to skirt around her toward the exit.

"You're here with Talan, aren't you?" she asked.

I turned to her. "I am. I'm Cora."

"I'm Tabitha." She gave a catlike smile, and there was something fierce in the curve of her lips. "I've never known Talan to take a woman to a party before. He's more the type to enjoy our company in private." Her smile broadened, and I was pretty sure I read something else there.

I frowned. "Are you telling me that you slept with my mate?"

Her eyes widened in shock. Clearly, she hadn't been expecting me to go straight for the jugular. She wanted to needle me with innuendos, ones that polite society wouldn't directly discuss. Too bad for her that I wasn't polite society.

"Why yes, actually." She leaned against the bathroom sink, a practiced pose that presented her curves to the best advantage. I wasn't into women, but even I could see that she had an absolutely stunning figure.

How was I supposed to compete with that?

I shook myself inwardly. I didn't want to compete

with her. Nothing could ever happen between Talan and me—it would be a terrible idea. I was looking for independence, not to be bound down again. Not to be controlled by fate. The fact that I was reacting so much to the idea of us being a couple was clearly insanity.

"Well, he's with me now, isn't he?" I turned and left. She didn't need to know that it was all fake. But I wanted to wipe that smile off her face, and I had.

As soon as I rejoined the party, Talan found me. He'd been waiting near the bathrooms, clearly not wanting me to be on my own for long.

"Is everything all right?" he asked.

"Totally fine. Just met one of your former lovers, though. Next time, warn me."

His brows drew together. "Tabitha. It was just a night."

"Well, it's still on Tabatha's mind."

Behind Talan, the doors to the main room opened wide, and the trumpet sounded. I shot him a look, brows raised. "An actual trumpet? Really?"

"Shh." He wrapped an arm around my shoulders and turned to face the doors as the queen entered. I knew the arm was just for show, but it still sent heat racing through me.

The queen was dressed in the most glorious gown, sparkling black lace that contrasted magnificently with her blond hair and showed hints of skin pale as snow. She smiled as she looked around the room, her gaze landing on us. A cunning glint entered her eyes, and she glided toward us. I'd never seen anybody so graceful before. She had to be using magic to move like that.

She stopped in front of us, a smile curving her lips. "I'm so glad you could make it."

"Thank you for the invitation." Talan nodded down toward me and squeezed his arm tighter. "And thank you for knocking some sense into me."

The queen laughed, a little too loudly.

"I don't believe you've met Cora?" Talan said.

I smiled and held out my hand. She looked down at it but didn't take it. Shit. Was I supposed curtsy or something?

She ignored my hand, but deigned to say, "It is lovely to meet you."

I didn't believe her for a second, but I wasn't particularly thrilled to be meeting her, either. She didn't have a drink in her hand, and I didn't want to give up an opportunity to slip her the truth potion. I smiled at her, trying to look as innocent as possible. "Can I get you a drink? You shouldn't be empty-handed at your own party."

"Oh, I'm fine. We're going into dinner now. There will be wine there."

I tried not to let the disappointment show on my face as I said, "Excellent. I'm starving."

She turned and drifted toward another set of doors on the opposite side of the room. One of the uniformed men rang a small silver bell and announced that dinner would be served.

We followed the crowd out of the room and onto an enormous wooden balcony that had been built amongst the treetops. Whatever mosquitoes should have lived in the Bayou had obviously been repelled by magic and replaced with tiny white moths that fluttered overhead, their white wings glinting in the moonlight. A long table in the middle was draped in white linen and flowers, spindly golden chairs pushed up to the edges. Talan and I tried to get a seat near the queen, but tiny name cards sat at each plate, and we found ours next to the creepy vampire couple. Oh, joy.

The meal passed slowly as the raucous laughter of the group grew louder. But I couldn't deny that the food was some of the best I'd ever eaten, and so was the drink. I sipped sparingly from my glass, though, and I spent most of the meal plotting how we could get the queen alone.

When it was over, the group retired back to the room where cocktails had been served.

I leaned close to Talan. "This is our chance."

"I'll see if I can bring her a drink."

Before he could reach the bar, the queen's spokesman rang his tiny silver bell again and pitched his voice over the crowd. "The queen will be retiring for the evening. Tomorrow will start early with our revelry and games. Should you want to compete, I advise that you seek your slumber soon."

Shit. Double shit.

I met Talan's gaze through the crowd. He turned and left the bar, joining me empty-handed. "Why don't we go to bed. We can talk there."

Go to bed.

Fates, I hoped there wasn't only one.

13

Cora

I followed Talan into a beautifully decorated bedchamber. Huge arched windows provided a view of the forest surrounding us, though not much was visible through the gloom—just flashes of trees under the moonlight.

Our luggage waited at the foot of the bed, which was an enormous thing covered in fluffy white bedding. And there was only one, of course.

Just my luck.

My gaze flicked toward Talan. "Seriously? One bed?"

"We won't be sleeping."

"What are you thinking?"

He approached me, his stride that of a predator. A

shiver ran down my spine as he crowded me against the wall. The movement was overtly sexual, and the heat in his eyes made a delicious shiver run through me.

He tipped his head toward my ear and whispered so quietly that I almost couldn't hear him, "The room could be monitored."

Of course. I didn't know the queen well, but I wouldn't put it past her. I moved my lips closer to his ear. To make it look more realistic, I wrapped my arms around his neck. If anyone was watching, I was going to give them a good show. "Do you have a plan?"

Talan dipped his head to brush his lips across my neck, right below my ear. I shivered. Had that been entirely necessary?

Honestly, I didn't care. I hoped he did it again.

"We sneak into her room and dose her with the truth potion," he murmured, low. "I don't want to stay here for the entire party. We need our answers sooner, so we'll have to go get them."

"I like it." I didn't bother to whisper that part. If anybody was watching, they would assume I liked his hands on me. Despite the high stakes and danger, or maybe because of them, my heart was racing. Being pressed up against Talan clouded my thoughts and made me want to kiss him.

"Cora." The words escaped Talan on a groan. "We shouldn't."

"Why not?" I couldn't believe I was saying it, especially after what had just happened between us, but I meant it. It would help solidify our alibi if someone was watching, and we needed to give the queen time to fall asleep. That would be my excuse. I tilted my head and pressed my lips to his.

It was as intoxicating as ever. Talan rumbled low in his throat and turned the tables on me, taking control. I loved it. His hands ran from my waist down to my hips, and he gripped them tightly, hoisting me up. I wrapped my legs around his waist and tightened my arms around his neck, surrendering to the passion of his kiss.

He towered over me, his size an aphrodisiac of its own. He kissed like a man starving for me. His lips and tongue and teeth drove me mindless with pleasure, and when he dragged his mouth to my neck, I cried out with a low whimper. "Talan. More."

"Yes. Anything." He growled low in his throat.

I ground my hips against his, lost to the delicious friction. He moved in a rhythm that drove all conscious thought from my mind. Soon, I wasn't in the queen's palace anymore—I was alone with Talan in a world that was entirely ours. He drove me out of my head with pleasure.

When he pulled back, I was panting and mindless.

"As much as I want to continue this, it's not the place," he whispered against my ear. "When I finally have you, I want it to be just us."

Oh, right. It was possible—probable—that we were

being watched. I didn't have much of a voyeur streak in me and wasn't keen on it.

I nodded, closing my eyes, and tried to catch my breath.

Gently, Talan lowered me to the ground. He stepped away, and the loss of his touch chilled me.

It was for the best, though.

I looked at the clock over the mantle and felt my jaw slacken. "Is it really after one o'clock?"

"It is. Time passes quickly when we're..."

Seriously. We'd arrived at eleven thirty. I hadn't realized so much time had passed. On the plus side, the queen was probably asleep. I moved my gaze toward the door and asked him, "Shall we?"

Talan

I nodded and pulled myself away from Cora. The loss of her touch made me ache, but I shoved the thought aside and walked to the door. I listened for a moment, finding it silent outside, then stepped out and let her follow me. In the hall, I turned and whispered, "Are you armed?"

"Of course."

"Good. We'll have to be quick. If someone was monitoring our room, they may be curious about why we left."

She nodded. "Do you know the way?"

"I do. Follow me." I set off through the castle, sticking to the shadows. Cora followed silently, light on her feet. We made it down to the main floor without meeting anyone.

On the landing, I looked out toward the rest of the castle. So much of it was open-air, with spiraling wooden staircases leading up to towers. The towers themselves were little more than platforms with wooden arches supporting the roofs.

It was beautiful, but it had to take a massive amount of magic to keep the climate temperate and the bugs away. The Bayou was the last place on Earth I would build a home, but the fae were determined.

"Do you know which way to go?" Cora asked.

"She's at the far end." Through the maze of twisting wooden paths and spiraling staircases, I could just make out the queen's tower. I'd never been there, but when I'd first moved to New Orleans, I'd done extensive research into the homes of all the most powerful supernaturals in the area. I had a vague idea of the layout from stories told by past guests.

Not that I needed it. Her tower was the largest, most ostentatious one. Three massive pennants wafted in the breeze, each studded with jewels that glittered under the light of the moon.

"Oh, yeah," Cora said. "I didn't even need to ask."

"Stay alert. As we get closer to her quarters, there will be protections in place." I started forward, moving silently down the path.

Cora stuck close to my side, her weapon gripped in her hand, a short, curved blade with a loop that hooked around her forefinger. The little dagger was a genius weapon, allowing her to punch, slice, and stab. I wondered for the hundredth time where she had learned her skills, and why she had needed them.

I shook the thought away—I needed to be on the alert, not wondering about the woman at my side.

The bottom part of the castle was quiet as we walked through the halls. Huge arched windows provided a view of the Bayou, and many of the glass panes were thrown open to let the warm air inside.

We were nearly to the queen's part of the castle when I sensed a guard ahead. If I focused closely, I could make out the sound of his breathing. Cora shot me a pointed look, then nodded toward the bend in the hall where the guard was likely stationed. I nodded, indicating that I knew what she was talking about, and pointed to myself.

I'll take him, I mouthed.

She shrugged and gestured for me to go ahead.

I slipped quietly down the hall, planning my attack. I would have to be careful—my usual fire magic wouldn't be practical in a wooden castle. Though I was sure it had been enchanted to repel normal fire, my demon fire would be far too strong. If I burned the place to the ground, we would certainly lose the element of surprise.

I slipped around the corner, immediately spotting the guard keeping watch over the intersection that led to the queen's quarters. His eyes widened when he saw me, and he lunged forward. I deflected his punch and grabbed him by the arm, spinning him around to trap him against my body. I pressed my fingertips to his temple and used my magic to command, "You will fall asleep."

He sagged in my arms, and I dragged his body to an alcove. A statue of a stallion reared on powerful hind legs. I stashed the unconscious fae behind the pedestal and turned to Cora.

She raised a brow. "Nice work. How long will he be out?"

"We have about an hour."

"Good. Let's move." She waited for me to lead the way, and I set off down the hall. There was another guard up ahead, and I used the same maneuver to take him out. I hid his body inside a small room and returned to Cora.

"This is a little too easy," she murmured, her tone wary.

"Maybe I'm just skilled." I grinned. "More likely, it will get worse the closer we get."

"Could be both."

Surprise flashed through me, followed by a low laugh.

Cora herself seemed a little shocked, as if she hadn't expected to joke with me. She turned and headed toward the queen's tower, stopping at the base of the stairs, a magnificent expanse of golden oak. Each step was fifteen feet wide, creating a massive spiral to the chamber at the top. There were no railings or walls at the edges, but fairy lights glittered all the way up, floating in the air.

We began to climb, staying side by side. About a quarter of the way up, vines suddenly sprouted between the stairs, wrapping around Cora's legs. It happened so quickly that she stumbled.

Two more vines wrapped around my ankles, and I drew a dagger from the ether.

"Shit!" Cora hissed. She sliced at the vines with her blade, moving so swiftly that her hands were almost a blur. "They're getting stronger the longer they stay on!"

She was right. The ones that clung to my legs had grown tighter and more persistent. Cora was so quick with her blade that she managed to free herself and leap up the stairs to escape. Her knife skills were phenomenally good, almost otherworldly.

"Here, let me help." Cora stepped down the stairs to rejoin me, but I threw out a hand.

"No! Get back." I didn't want her to get hurt on my

account. I gave up with the knife and gripped one of the vines in my hands. Carefully, I sent a tiny bit of my fire magic into the thick stem. It shriveled away, crumbling in my grasp.

Thank fates.

Within moments, I burned away the rest of the vines and joined Cora on the steps above.

"Let's hurry," she whispered, turning to run up the stairs.

We encountered no more obstacles until we reached the top. Two guards stood at either side of the door, their hands clasped in front of them and their stony gazes straight ahead.

As soon as we appeared at the top of the stairs, they stiffened, their eyes widening. They lunged into action but were too slow. I sent a persuasive blast of magic directly into their chests, a difficult bit of magic that I didn't often use. They stopped dead in their tracks. Eyes rolling back in their heads, they collapsed.

"Nicely done," Cora murmured.

"Let's hope I don't need much more magic. That sapped a lot of it." I'd need to rest before I attempted anything so difficult again. Sometimes, the subtlest magics were the most difficult.

"Don't worry, I've got your back." She grinned at me. "Now let's go get the queen."

∽

Cora

I crept into the queen's room, my footsteps silent on the thick rugs. Talan finished binding the guards, then followed close behind me.

With the guards subdued out in the hall, we were alone with the queen. She lay asleep in the bed, still as a statue.

I moved to her side, staring down at her. Honestly, this kind of thing gave me the creeps. I felt like a stalker. But we needed our answers, and if she was to blame, people could die because of her. I drew the anti-magic cuffs from my pocket and handed them to Talan, suddenly grateful that my old boss had sent the accountant after me. Having these things was going to turn out very handy.

Talan took the cuffs and nodded, moving to stand by her waist. I drew a bottle of truth potion from my pocket and uncorked it, catching his gaze. We'd need to time this perfectly.

The queen lay on her back, glowing with an unusual, ethereal beauty. She slept with her mouth closed, which wasn't ideal, but I could fix that.

Ready? I mouthed.

Talan nodded.

I tickled the queen's lip with the tip of my finger, and she gasped. When her mouth opened, I emptied the contents of the vial between her lips. She sputtered and sat up, blinking wildly in the gloom. Talan slapped the cuffs around her wrists, suffocating her magic.

Her gaze landed on us, rage flashing in her eyes. "How dare you sneak into my quarters and accost me."

I shrugged. "That was a truth potion I just fed you. We won't hurt you, but we will be asking questions. Don't even try to lie. The potion will make it impossible."

I stepped aside to let Talan move forward. He would be the one asking the questions since it was his home at risk.

"Guards!" she screeched. Her eyes were fiery with anger as they landed on me. "When they get here, we'll string you up and watch you hang." She sounded so vicious that I believed her.

"There are no guards outside to hear," Talan said. "But don't worry, we didn't kill them."

"I don't care," she hissed. "You're dead for this. I swear on my kingdom that I'll have your head, no matter what it takes."

I shot Talan a glance, a bit nervous about the vehemence in her voice. She really would kill us, that was for sure. I'd never seen anyone so enraged or determined.

"There are more guards in the castle." She glared at us. "They will come."

"Then we had better be quick," Talan said. "Is it your

magic in my house that's manipulating the Well of Souls?"

The queen pinched her lips closed, but her face darkened until it was nearly maroon. Finally, she spat out the word, "Yes. But if you think I want to steal your part of New Orleans, you're sorely mistaken. We have no desire to live there."

Well, that was more information than I'd expected to get. It also confused matters more. But the truth potion wouldn't work indefinitely. Depending upon how strong the queen was, the truth potion would only get three or four questions out of her. Maybe less, maybe more. Talan had to focus on the most important things first.

"How do we stop it?" Talan asked.

"*You* can't stop it." She gave an evil grin. "At least, not that I know of."

"How is that even—"

I gripped Talan's arms to keep him from finishing the question. From the harsh, frustrated tone of his voice, it was clear he wanted to ask how it was possible she didn't know how to break her own spell. That wasn't the information we needed.

"Who can break the spell then?" I asked. "Because someone has to be able to."

"The one who cast it." She said the words so easily that I knew the truth potion was starting to wear off. She could likely feel it weakening, and she wasn't afraid of saying too much.

"Who cast the spell?" Talan asked.

"One of your kind." She grinned. "I think the potion has worn off. But don't bother running away. We will hunt you. Save me the trouble and stay until the guards get here."

"Who deployed the spell?" Talan demanded.

She pinned her lips shut, desperate not to answer. Though her face turned red, she didn't reach the deep shade of maroon she had before.

"She's fighting off the potion. I think it really has worn off." I looked toward the door, wondering when her backup would arrive. Even though the guards in the hallway were unconscious, her confidence made me wary. She knew that her scream had reached someone. "We need to get out of here."

"Fine," Talan said. "But she's coming with us."

I gasped, and the queen squawked.

Talan plunged a hand into his pocket and withdrew three glass vials, then handed one to me. "Here, drink. It's an invisibility potion."

He uncorked one of the bottles and moved toward the queen to pour it down her throat. She thrashed, trying to break away from him, but without her magic, she wasn't particularly strong.

I uncorked the bottle and was about to toss the liquid down my throat when the door was shoved open. Four fae guards rushed into the room, raising their hands, and blasting us with a bright white light. We were thrown back against the wall, and the glass vial flew from my hand, shattering against the ground. Every bone in my body ached as I rose up on my elbows and stared at them, my vision hazy from the force of the magic.

Next to me, the queen was unconscious, and Talan was staggering to his feet. She'd clearly been hit by mistake, and I dreaded to think what would happen to the guards who'd screwed that up.

Before I could rise, the guards threw another blast of magic straight at me, and it was the last thing I remembered.

14

Cora

I awoke in a cell, head aching and vision blurry. I blinked, and my surroundings came into focus.

What the hell?

This was like no cell I'd ever seen before. There were no stone walls, no rats, no putrid water dripping from the ceiling. Instead, it was a wooden platform high amongst the trees. The arched windows revealed a view of the forest beyond, which was cast in the shadow created by a partial moon. Magic sparked around the edges of the window, a sharp prickling that promised death if I so much as touched it.

I tried to draw my knife from the ether, but a spell blocked it. Damn it.

Next to me, Talan lay unconscious on the smooth wooden floorboards. The anti-magic cuffs bound his wrists. Fear spiked, and I leaned over to shake his shoulder. "Talan, wake up."

He groaned low but didn't open his eyes. What had they hit him with? It had to have been something powerful. They knew how strong he was—they would have made sure to take him out.

Thank fates they hadn't known what I was capable of.

Talan moaned again, then opened his eyes, his gaze unfocused. He blinked to clear his vision.

"Cora?" His voice was rough with worry and pain. "Are you all right?"

"Yeah, yeah. I'm good. How are you?"

"Fine." He rubbed his head and sat up. "Whatever they used was strong, though. How long was I out?"

"No idea. I was out, too." I looked out the windows again. It was still full dark, so it couldn't have been that long. "We're in some kind of weird cell. Did the queen mean what she said about killing us?"

"Absolutely." He frowned. "Especially with the state the queen is in. There's something off about her. She's more unhinged, and her power is more intense, though I can't put my finger on why."

I swallowed hard. Attempting to kidnap the queen was pretty damned bad. Probably the worst crime one could attempt, short of murder. She was definitely going to kill us.

And we were totally trapped. The magic that sparked at the windows and door made it clear we weren't getting out until someone came to get us.

I drew in an unsteady breath as the walls seemed to close in on me. It didn't matter that the cell was airy and spacious--it was being trapped that bothered me. I shivered, memories of my time in captivity making anxiety claw at my skin.

Talan's gaze sharpened on me and worry creased his brow. "What's wrong?"

"Nothing. Just don't like being locked in a cell, that's all." I rubbed my arms as if I could infuse them with warmth, even though the air around me was plenty warm.

"I know what you mean." There was something in his voice that made me think he really did.

"What do you mean?" How could someone as powerful as him know what it was like to be a captive, forced to fight for someone you hated?

"Just that I hate being locked up."

"Yeah, but it sounded like there was more to it."

His gaze cut toward mine, then away. There was definitely something there.

"Tell me." I wanted to know—desperately. It wasn't just about seeking a distraction from my fear and misery. I wanted to know him better. I shouldn't have sought something like that, but I couldn't help myself.

He frowned, watching the door. When it was clear that no one was coming up the stairs at that moment, he spoke. "I'll tell you what you want to know if you'll tell me why those men attacked you in New York."

I didn't want to confide in him, but I desperately wanted to know more about him. I twisted my hands together, weighing my options. Maybe it was the stress of the day. Maybe it was because I was freaked out about being in the tower. Whatever it was, it was enough to make me want to spill my guts.

So I did.

"I was raised in an orphanage that trained mercenaries. Then I was sold to a bastard who made me work as an assassin."

Shock flashed in his eyes, along with anger. "Who was it?"

I waved a hand. "Doesn't matter. I escaped."

"It *does* matter. I'll kill them."

I felt a reluctant smile cross my face. "Really?"

I believed him, so I don't know why I asked. Probably shock. I hadn't expected him to care so much. At all, really, but from the vehemence in his voice, he cared a hell of a lot.

"Just tell me where he is." The growl in his voice made me even happier, weird as that was. I liked having someone on my side. I hadn't expected it, but now that it was happening, I was a big fan.

"New York, obviously. But we'll worry about that later." I nudged his shoulder. "I want to know why you're so familiar with being locked up. Why does it seem like there's history here?"

"Rathbine isn't just a colleague. When I was a teenager, he forced me to fight in his gladiator ring. Battles to the death."

Horror opened a chasm in my chest. "What?"

"Demons can be monsters."

"No kidding. But you escaped." It was more question than statement, but I was too stunned to put the right inflection on it.

He nodded. "I did. And I created my part of New Orleans afterward. I've wanted to kill Rathbine ever since, but the Council of Demons prohibits it. They would come after my people if I committed a crime like that."

Shit. That was terrible. "I can't believe you've had a worse life than me."

"I'd say we're about equal on the misery scale." His face darkened. "And if I can't kill my captor, at least I can kill yours."

I smiled, some vicious part of me rejoicing. I didn't like that part of myself, but it was there all the same. I tried to tamp it down, and I succeeded a bit.

"Well, I'd like to kill Rathbine." I frowned. Hmm.

That wasn't any less vicious than my pleasure over Talan wanting to kill my old captor.

I'd have to work on that.

"We need to be ready when they come for us," Talan said. "Assume they'll kill us and do whatever it takes to get free."

I nodded, not liking the idea of it. I knew what my *whatever it takes* was, and it was pretty ugly. I still wasn't sure if Talan had seen how I'd killed my attacker from earlier today, but I didn't want him to know what I was capable of.

He looked down at his wrists, grimacing. "These are powerful."

"They must have taken them off the queen and put them on you." They hadn't bound me, though. Must not think I was much of a threat.

Good.

The sound of footsteps echoed on the stairs, and we stood. We faced the door, having no time to move aside. It swung open, and two guards entered. They held massive shields in front of them, their gazes riveted to Talan. He had no magic as long as he wore the cuffs, but they were right to be afraid of him. He was deadly all the same.

"It's time for you to swing." The ice in the guard's voice sent a shiver down my spine.

"Swing?" I asked. "As in hang?"

Both guards nodded, and the excitement in their

eyes made my stomach lurch. The one on the left gave a sickening grin and said, "I'd like to do it myself, but the queen wants to watch."

"She's gone mad," Talan said. "And so have you."

He was right. As I studied the guards, there was the glint of madness in their eyes. Or perhaps they'd always been bloodthirsty.

Either way, it didn't matter. If they took us to the queen, we would be dead.

And if we were dead, then there would be no one to tell the others what we'd learned here. Talan's entire community was at risk.

"Come on." The guard on the left gestured at me. "Dawdling isn't going to change your fate."

I walked toward them, my skin going cold at the knowledge of what I was about to do. I hated to use my power like this, but I couldn't think of another way.

I swallowed hard, a buzzing sound in my head. When I reached the guards and raised my hand and faltered.

I can't do it.

Not if they didn't see it coming. It felt too evil. I always gave my opponents a fighting chance.

So, I lashed out with my foot instead, hoping that I could fight them into submission. My heel collided with the shins of the guy on the right. He went down hard, his sword clattering to the ground.

Talan lunged for the other guard, colliding with him

in a pile on the ground. He swung hard for the other man's face, but I couldn't take the time to watch.

I needed a weapon, but the spell blocked me from drawing my own. I darted toward the fallen guard and wrapped my hand around the hilt of the dagger strapped to his leg.

I yanked it out and darted backwards. He staggered to his feet, and I lunged for him, swiping across his chest. He was too fast, and the blade barely nicked him. He swung his shield toward me, aiming for my head. I lunged to the side, taking the blow to my shoulder. I dropped the dagger and whirled to face him, my arm dead from the pain.

He charged me, the gleam of bloodlust bright in his eyes. I had nowhere to go. Behind me, the windows had been enchanted to maim anyone who touched them. No escape there.

The guard reached for my throat and gripped me hard. Flashbacks to the moment where I had nearly died in the alley filled my mind. I panicked and reached out to grab his hand, feeding my magic into him. He collapsed like a stone, his grip leaving my throat. I gasped and staggered away from the window.

When I looked up, Talan was watching me. He stood over the body of the other fallen guard, a frown on his face. There were a dozen questions in his eyes, but the most important one was obvious.

How did you kill him?

"We'll talk about it later," I said. "Look for a key to those cuffs." I bent and searched the body of the man I'd killed. Guilt streaked through me, but it wasn't as bad as if I'd killed him without warning. He'd attacked first, and I'd snapped into action. I would have to keep telling myself that.

I patted down his clothing, looking for the key, but had no luck.

"I've got it." Talan's words made relief rush through me. I rose to my feet and hurried toward him, holding out my hand. He handed me the key, and I used it to unlock his shackles. He handed me the cuffs and shook his wrists. I tucked them in my pocket and looked down at the guard at his feet.

"Not dead," he said.

"I wish I could say the same for mine."

"He was going to kill you. Don't feel guilty."

I ignored his words and headed toward the door. We needed to make it out of there before the queen realized we hadn't showed up at her hanging tree on time. The stairs that spiraled down around the tower were narrow and had no railing.

Just my luck.

My stomach pitched as I took them two at a time, moving as quickly as I could without freaking out. I'd never been a huge fan of heights, but this place was making me even more nervous than normal. Even the warmth of the night air was claustrophobic.

"I hate it out here," I muttered. I just wanted to get back to the city.

We were about halfway down the stairs when two more guards appeared below us. They stopped as soon as they saw us, raising their swords and pinning us with identical glares. Outside the cell, I was able to draw my dagger from the ether. It was unnecessary, though.

Talan lifted his hands. Green fire twisted around his wrists, stretching from his palms to wrap around the men. They shrieked, pain twisting their features.

"Come on." Talan grabbed my hand and dragged me down the stairs past the men. "They'll survive."

I was glad. I didn't like what they were doing to us, but I couldn't be sure they were doing it of their own free will or at the behest of their queen.

We reached the base of the stairs and sprinted into the depths of the Bayou, getting as far away from the castle as we could. The Bayou whispered with threat, and I could feel it pressing in on us from all directions.

"Do you know the way to the portal?" I asked.

"Roughly. This way." Talan ran between the trees, and I sprinted to keep up. He made sure to always stay close to me, and I was grateful. The wet ground sucked at my fancy shoes, slowing me down, and I cursed the fact that I'd dressed for the party and hadn't changed into more practical clothing.

Overhead, Spanish moss draped from the trees,

heavy and still in the quiet air, the sound of our labored breathing all the more apparent.

A shrieking noise sounded from a distance, high and foreign. Definitely not human.

"What is that?" I asked.

"Swamp banshees." Talan searched the sky, never slowing. "Don't let them touch you. Their touch causes great pain."

Lungs burning, I pushed myself to the limit. When pale white figures appeared at the corner of my vision, my adrenaline spiked higher.

We were too slow. The swamp banshees were on us in seconds, their ephemeral forms glimmering with pale white light. Ragged white dresses wafted around their bodies, and their dark hair floated in the air. They reached their skeletal hands toward us. Talan dodged, and I tried to strike out at the one who attacked me. My hand drifted through her form, and she cackled.

Agony shot through me.

I nearly went to my knees, and the swamp banshee grabbed me around the waist, hugging me tight. Pain, unbelievable pain, rushed through me, making bile rise in my throat. The strength leached from me as the banshee drew it into herself.

Her shrieks echoed in my head, so loud that they drowned out all thought. Instinct drove me. I grabbed her, feeding as much of my deadly magic into her as I could. The pain was enough to steal my vision, but her screams stopped, and her grip slackened. Soon, she was no longer holding me, and I was able to open my eyes.

My attacker was gone, but the other banshee had her arms wrapped tight around Talan. He was pale, his features drawn tight with pain. I lunged for them, grabbing his attacker by her shoulders, and feeding my magic into her. She withered before my eyes, and it took everything I had to stay on my feet, the pain of contact with her dulling my senses.

Soon, she let go of Talan and shot toward the sky, disappearing as quickly as she'd come.

I gasped, going to my knees. My breathing slowed as the anguish faded. Talan helped me to my feet, his face still pale and drawn. His pupils were blown wide with agony, but within seconds, they had shrunk back to their normal size.

"Are you all right?" he asked.

I dragged a shaky hand through my hair. "Yeah, surprisingly."

"Their effect is short-lived, as long as you can get away from them. Which normally, a person can't." He gave me a loaded look. He wanted to know how I'd gotten them to leave us alone, but I shook my head. Mercifully, he left it at that, saying simply, "Thank you."

"Anytime. Now lead the way. I want to get out of here."

Talan turned and set off through the swamp. I followed, the ground getting wetter and wetter as we trekked through the Bayou. The feeling of squelching mud between my toes made my stomach turn, but I kept going, focusing on getting the hell out of there.

When I caught a glimpse of glowing eyes, brilliant yellow orbs low to the ground and impossible to miss, my skin chilled.

Gators.

There had to be at least a dozen pairs, and they were moving closer. Quickly.

"Talan, do you see that?" I picked up the pace, sticking close to him.

"I do. Keep moving."

The creatures were fast, their stubby legs eating up the ground as they charged. As they neared, I realized there wasn't a single one under fifteen feet long. They snapped massive jaws filled with vicious-looking teeth.

Talan raised his arms, and fire formed a ring around us. The green flame drove the creatures back, and we kept moving. Talan kept the protective barrier roaring as we walked. I'd have been worried about a forest fire, except for the fact that the swamp was soaking wet.

"We're almost there," Talan said. "We should see the gate any minute."

He was right. Through the wall of flame, I spotted the silver gate ahead. There had to be twenty guards standing at the gate, barring our way through the portal back to Earth.

Despair shot through me. "We can't fight all of them."

Talan cursed low. "It's the only portal."

"Can we create a distraction?"

"We're going to have to."

I had no idea what could possibly work, though. More flame? Would that draw enough of the guards?

And then I saw them, three figures on the other side of the gate, their forms blessedly familiar. Mia, Rei, and Calex.

Holy fates. My friends came for me.

Joy flared.

Calex's voice carried across the swamps. "We are here for Talan and Cora. They were supposed to check in hours ago, and they did not. We demand that you bring them to us, or you will feel the wrath of New Orleans."

I looked at Talan, my brows raised. "Is that a thing?"

He nodded sharply. "Calex represents Enforcement. There's a treaty between the fae and the citizens of New Orleans. We aren't to harm each other, or there will be consequences."

"So, this could work?"

He nodded curtly, his gaze glued to the group ahead.

"We have no idea who you're talking about," shouted the lead guard.

"Yes, you do." The steel in Calex's voice was evident. "I demand you release them to us."

The guards murmured to each other, but before they could respond, Talan grabbed my hand and pulled me forward. We strode toward the gate, my heart fluttering with nerves.

"We need to call the queen to let her know you're here," the guard said to Calex.

Before he could, Talan and I reached them.

"Thank you for coming," Talan said. "You'll have to forgive us. We were having such a good time that we forgot to check in with you. We're ready to leave, though."

The guards looked between us and Calex. I looked up at Talan, wondering what his angle was.

"Good." Calex gestured to the guard "Open the gate."

The guard frowned and shook his head. "Not without the queen's permission."

"You know that holding them unwillingly will cause a war," Calex said.

"Betraying my queen will cause my death."

From behind us, I felt a wave of power rush over me. The queen.

My skin chilled. I turned to see her gliding toward us, moving so gracefully she might as well have been floating. Her glittering dressing gown swept the ground beneath her, and she raised a graceful hand to wave at the guard. "I appreciate your loyalty," she said. "However, you may open the gate and allow our guests to leave."

She wasn't willing to do anything in front of Calex,

but I could read the message in her gaze like it was written in stone.

It's not over.

Ice skated up my spine as I watched the guard open the gate. I looked back at the queen, studying her face.

Talan was right—there was a hint of madness to her. I just wanted to get the hell out of there before she went back on her word and attacked.

The gate opened, and we strode through. My friends grabbed my hands and pulled me away. I glanced over my shoulder to see the queen watching us, her eyes glinting with cunning.

Yes, this was far from over.

15

Cora

After we left the fae realm, we headed directly back to my place. Calex dropped Mia, Rei, Talan, and me at the front door of the bookstore.

I leaned down to meet his gaze. "Thank you. Seriously."

He nodded. "Anytime."

As he pulled away from the curb, Mia and Rei waved goodbye and headed down the street. They planned to get cleaned up at their own places, then reconvene later.

I entered the bookstore and staggered up the stairs to the top floor apartment. Talan followed me, and I was too tired to ask him why. Mostly, I just wanted to see Fiona and make sure she was okay.

As I stepped into the apartment, my gaze went immediately to my ghost friend. She was curled on the couch. Her eyes lit up when she saw me, and she leapt up. "Cora! I'm so glad you're back. Are you okay? Rei and Mia ran off a little while ago to find you."

"I'm fine."

"Well, tell me what happened." Fiona looked between me and Talan, curiosity in her eyes.

I raised a finger and said, "Hold that thought. I need a shower."

Fiona groaned but gestured for me to hurry to the shower. "You're right. I can't argue with that. You smell like the swamp."

I hurried past her, spotting Balthazar sitting on top of his toaster, which sat on the little wooden table next to the couch. It was plugged in beneath the table, and he was purring contentedly as it baked him from underneath. Just the sight of him made me even happier to be home.

I shut myself into the little bathroom and stripped off my clothes, then cranked on the shower. I jumped in without waiting for it to get warm, shuddering as the cold droplets cascaded down on my head. It felt like hell, but I didn't mind. Anything to get the disgusting swamp off of me as quickly as possible.

Unfortunately, the outfit that Mia had lent me was destroyed. Not to mention, I'd lost all the luggage I'd left behind. Guilt tugged at me. I'd have to find a way to replace it all.

That was a problem for another time, though. I showered as quickly as I could, then threw on a bathrobe and returned to the living room.

Talan was still there, standing on a section of wooden flooring that wouldn't suffer from his muddy boots. I raised a brow at him. "I thought you would leave once you dropped me off."

He shook his head. "The queen will come for us eventually. I'm not leaving you alone."

Shit. After everything that had happened between us, I didn't know if I could handle being alone with him. On the other hand, he was right. The queen was massively powerful and pissed as hell at us.

But still... It was strange to have him in my home. I actually kind of liked it, and that scared the hell out of me. It was way too close to caring for him. "Couldn't you post some guards outside like you did before?"

"I already did. But I'm staying inside with you."

My mind spun. There was too much at stake. Now wasn't the time for me to get picky. Anyway, I appreciated the extra protection. I wasn't stupid.

"Fine, thank you." I pointed to the bathroom. "If you're going to stay, then get in the shower."

"Gladly." He took off his boots and moved past me toward the bathroom.

Exhausted, I curled up on the corner of the sofa.

Fiona stayed on her side, and Balthazar pressed a paw onto the toaster lever to heat it back up.

"Oh, my God, I'm exhausted." I leaned back against the cushions and closed my eyes.

"Talan gave me a brief rundown," Fiona said. "So, you think the queen has something to do with it?"

"Yep, but she has a partner somewhere. Likely a demon from Talan's past named Rathbine."

The doorbell rang, and I looked at Fiona. "Who's that?"

"Probably Liora. He called her. Told her to pick up takeout for you and deliver some clothes for him."

At the sound of takeout, my stomach rumbled. I was starving. "How did he get takeout at this hour? It's close to dawn."

"He's the demon lord. Someone opened their shop for him."

Hmm. That was a perk.

I rose from the couch and headed downstairs to the bookshop, opening the door to reveal Liora standing between two hulking men. She raised a plastic bag and a smaller canvas bag.

"Thank you." I took the bags. "Do you want to come in? The more the merrier, at this point."

She shook her head. "I'm gonna keep an eye on things from out here. But thanks."

I nodded. "Thanks again."

I headed upstairs with my loot and tossed the

clothes into the bathroom. Talan was still in the shower. Though I couldn't see him behind the ratty shower curtain, my imagination was working just fine, and my cheeks heated. I waited until the heat faded, then returned to the living room.

Fiona leaned forward and sniffed the air. "What did he order?"

She couldn't eat, but she was definitely still interested in food. It did smell divine.

I pulled out the container and opened it up to reveal Pad Thai, one of my favorite dishes. I dug in with the borrowed chopsticks and was halfway done by the time Talan appeared back in the living room.

I looked down at the couch. "I guess I'm sitting on your bed."

Even as I said it, a huge part of me wanted to invite him to my bed so that he could hold me as I fell asleep. It sounded purely divine, but it was a terrible idea. Not just because I didn't want to fall for him, but because he'd seen me kill a person with my touch. I couldn't handle questions right now.

Fiona and I rose, and she gestured to the couch like he was the prizewinner on a game show. "If you're lucky, Balthazar will sleep on your head."

"Just how I like it," Talan said.

A surprised laugh huffed out of me. I set the half-finished Thai container on the table and pointed to it. "Help yourself. And thanks. I appreciate it."

He nodded and approached the couch.

I hurried to the bedroom door. "I just need a little sleep. I'll see you in the morning."

As I shut the bedroom door behind me, I knew I'd made the right decision.

I woke to the alarm blaring in my ear, the sun warm on my face. Groggily, I threw the covers off and rose from the bed like a vampire from her slumber. I felt more like a zombie, though. Probably looked like one, too.

I'd only had a few hours' sleep, though I'd definitely needed more. But Fiona relied on me, and I needed to get back to work.

I threw on a change of clothes and headed into the living room. Instead of Talan, I found Liora on my couch. She was flipping through one of the magazines on the coffee table. She looked up when I entered the room.

"Where's Talan?" I asked.

"He's making arrangements to question Rathbine. Since I'm his best fighter, and you're his most valuable person, he's stationed me here."

Surprise flashed through me. "Most valuable person?"

Liora grinned. "You might not agree with it, but fate is certainly very clear about it. So is Talan."

"He hasn't said anything to me."

"Does he seem like the type?" Liora shrugged. "Anyway, actions speak louder than words. The fact that I'm here says it all."

Of course, a huge part of me liked that, but it also made me nervous. I was having a hard enough time adapting to having friends. Adapting to anything else would be emotional overload. "I need coffee. You want one?"

"Yeah, thanks." Liora picked up the magazine again and continued to peruse it.

I got to work making the coffee, wishing that I could run over to Mia's. There was no time, and if I were being honest, I was worried about being in the street. The fae queen was enraged, and I wouldn't be surprised if she had people waiting for me out there. I needed to stay free long enough to fix whatever was happening to Fiona.

Once the coffee was made, I brought a cup to Liora and sat on the couch next to her. I sipped, wincing at the heat, then sipped again. I needed the caffeine more than I needed working taste buds, and my coffee wasn't good, anyway.

A knock sounded on the door below.

"I'll get that." I brought my coffee with me as I hurried downstairs. I wasn't surprised to find Talan on the doorstep, and I let him in. "Do you know our next move?"

He nodded. "I've called an emergency meeting of the Demon Council, but we're going to need allies before we go. So, I'm going to visit a friend who will be able to help us."

"I'm coming."

"Underworlds aren't pleasant places. You should stay here."

"Nope. As long as Fiona is at risk, I'm going to be at the front of this." I glared at him to make sure he saw how serious I was.

The corner of his mouth twitched, and I couldn't tell if he was annoyed or impressed. Maybe both.

"Accept it, I'm coming," I said. "We're nearing our answers, I can feel it. I have to be there for Fiona. I can't fail at this."

"This means a lot to you," he said, his gaze searching mine.

I had no response—how was I supposed to explain what it was like to have a friend for the first time in my life? I couldn't. "I'm going to get my jacket."

I turned and hurried toward the stairs.

"You're a good friend." His voice followed me up the stairs, and the respect in it made me blush. It wasn't a compliment I'd ever gotten before, but I liked it.

I hurried into the living room and spotted Fiona coming out of the kitchen. "We've got another lead, and I'm going to go check it out," I said. "Liora, you can probably leave."

Liora stood. "Excellent. Talan is downstairs?"

I nodded. She hurried from the room. I looked at Fiona. "How do you feel?"

Fiona smiled, but it wasn't as broad as it normally was, and the shadows beneath her eyes looked darker. "I think it might be getting stronger. I can feel the portal pulling on me all the time now. I think it's our connection that keeps me here. Otherwise, I'd be gone."

I squeezed her hand. "Just hang in there. We've almost got our answers—I can feel it."

"Thank you." The tightness in Fiona's voice made tears prick my eyes. She was trying not to cry, and if I saw a single tear roll down her cheek, I would definitely lose it. I spun around and headed to the door. "I'll be back soon."

She said nothing, and I hurried down the stairs to join Talan and Liora, who stood by the door.

"Can we leave now?" I said. "We're running out of time."

"No kidding," Liora said. "There were ten more disappearances overnight."

This was getting so much worse.

"Come on," Talan said. "Markus is waiting."

Good—I just hoped Markus would be willing to help us.

16

Talan

I led Cora to the demon bar that contained the portal to Markus's underworld. Worry tugged at me, and I looked down at her. "Are you sure about this?"

She looked up at me, the sunlight glinting on her hair. "Definitely. Stop asking."

"Fine, but I'm not letting you out of my sight." I would worry about her, of course, but I was also fairly certain that I'd figured out what her magic was—she could kill with a touch.

The gift was rare—almost unheard of—and she worked hard to keep it a secret. She also only used it when she was backed into a corner and had no way out. I wasn't surprised. Cora was nothing if not ethical.

It also meant that she could defend herself in almost any circumstance. Especially if her attacker didn't know what she was capable of. She didn't want to talk about it, though, and I could respect that. I was just grateful she had that weapon in her arsenal.

We reached the dingy bar, and I entered before her. This place was often home to a rougher clientele, and I didn't want them to make her uncomfortable when she entered. If they saw me, they wouldn't dare.

Cora came in behind me. The interior of the bar was dark and gloomy, with the faint scent of brimstone hanging in the air. Brilliantly-colored liquor bottles lined the glass wall behind the bar, all of them imported from Markus's underworld. He specialized in producing liquors favored by demons, hence his portal being located in a bar.

I caught the bartender's eye and nodded toward the back where the portal was located. The bartender set down the glass she was cleaning and went to unlock the door.

"This way." I stayed close by Cora as I led her toward the back room.

I felt the gazes of the bar patrons on us as we walked, but no one said a word. There were a few murmurs of respectful greeting, but nothing more. Just how I liked it.

We reached the back door, and I led her into the room that contained the portal. It gleamed with a dull gray light, edged with a dark green glow. The bartender stood next to it, her gaze on me.

"Thank you, Troya." I nodded at her.

"He's not expecting anyone," Troya said. "Hopefully, he won't be a dick."

Markus was known to have a temper, but rarely with me. "It's fine."

"Good luck." She left the room, shutting and locking the door behind her.

"Is he a bastard?" Cora asked.

"No more so than me. And he's dangerous, but we've been friends a long time. If anybody can disturb his solitude without pissing him off, it's me."

"If you say so. But do you have a plan?"

"Yes. I'll tell you about it when we meet Markus." I held out my hand. "The portal will take us directly to his house. Don't let go."

She squeezed my hand. "Lead the way."

I stepped through, pulling her along with me. The ether sucked us in and spun us through space, eventually spitting us out on a glossy lawn. The grass itself was dark emerald, a cloak of velvet that led to a massive modern home. Markus had built it with the spoils of his enterprise and lived there alone. The structure was made entirely of glass and black granite, and it hung off the edge of the cliff over the crashing sea. The pale sun gleamed on the glass.

At my side, Cora gasped. "It's beautiful."

"Not all underworlds are so beautiful. Mine certainly isn't."

"Is that why you went to New Orleans?"

"One of the reasons, yes. I also didn't want to be anywhere near Rathbine."

"With any luck, we'll get rid of him for good. If he's behind this, you'll be able to get him off the Council, right?"

"More than that." I would kill him. At my side, I felt my fists clench. It took a conscious effort to relax them. "Come. We shouldn't linger out here."

As we neared the house, a herd of underworld horses galloped by us. Their bodies were made of bone and black flame, and their eyes burned with fire. They neighed a greeting, but it sounded more like a scream.

"Now that's what I was expecting from the underworld," Cora said.

I felt a reluctant smile tug at the corner of my mouth, then knocked on Markus's front door. It took only a moment for it to swing open. I nodded at the butler, and the demon inclined his head as he stepped aside to let us in.

"I will fetch the master." The butler's voice was a low murmur as he turned and headed into the house.

We waited in the massive foyer. A huge chandelier flickered overhead, flame twisting around the delicate wrought iron.

A few moments later, the butler reappeared at the far door. "You may come this way."

Cora and I walked toward him. I'd been in Markus's house several times before, and we were heading toward the main living space. As we entered the huge room, I spotted Markus standing in front of the massive glass wall that overlooked the sea.

He arched a brow. "I don't imagine this is a social call?"

"What gave it away?"

"The fact that you never visit." His gaze moved to Cora. "Although I didn't expect you to bring a companion."

The interest in his eyes made jealousy alight inside my chest, but I shoved it aside. "This is Cora. She's helping me with something that involves Rathbine, which is what we're here to discuss."

Shadows crossed Markus's face. I'd met him in the gladiator pit at Rathbine's estate, and he hated him as much as I did. It was why we were here to ask him for help—I knew he would agree.

"That bastard?" Markus asked.

"Unfortunately."

"It was only a matter of time before he became a real problem." Markus nodded toward a set of wide glass doors that led out onto a balcony. "This way."

We followed him outside. The sound of crashing

waves filled the air, and the sea sparkled in the distance. Markus led us to the large table in the center of the patio. He sat, and we joined him.

"What's Rathbine up to?" he asked.

"The portal that leads from Evonec to New Orleans is malfunctioning," I said. "Demons and ghosts are going missing as a result, and we think that Rathbine is to blame."

Markus frowned. "What's his goal?"

"We think he wants my part of New Orleans. If he can get rid of enough of my demons and have control of the portal, he'll manage it."

Markus leaned back and crossed his arms over his chest. "I get it. You want to accuse him in front of the Council, but you need proof."

"Exactly." The Council forbade accusations without proof. "Because we're running out of time, we need to move quickly. I called an emergency meeting tonight so that I could provide them with that evidence."

I could feel Cora's confused gaze on me. We didn't actually have the evidence, and she knew it.

"You have it?" Markus asked.

"No, and that's why I need your help. We have to get control of the Council and dose Rathbine with the truth potion that will force him to admit to what he's done in front of everyone."

Markus laughed. "How the hell do you plan to do

that? He won't take it willingly, and the other Council members won't force him if you don't already have proof."

"That's why we'll have to ask for forgiveness rather than permission, because the Council certainly won't grant it."

He shrugged. "True enough. So what's the plan?"

"We'll surprise Rathbine and the others. I can bind part of the Council with my demon fire, but not all of them. You're the only one as strong as me, so I need your help to bind the rest of them. While we do that, Cora will slip him the truth potion." I looked at Cora. "If you agree." I already knew she would. I'd tried to think of a way not to include her, but she would insist. It was just who she was. It scared the hell out of me because it put her in danger, but I couldn't control her.

"Of course." She gave me a look like I was crazy to think she wouldn't.

"It's dangerous there," Markus said. "And outsiders aren't invited."

"She'll take an invisibility potion so that she can dose him with the truth potion by surprise. With any luck, we'll get her out of there before the others notice. But if they do, they'll be so distracted by what Rathbine has done they won't have much time to be angry." And I would tear them apart if they threatened Cora.

I felt Markus's considering gaze on me and wondered if he could read my mind.

"All right. I'll help. Because I know you can't do it without me." Markus rose. "But we're going to need to go over the plan carefully."

"Thank you." I'd known I could count on him.

We discussed every element of the plan, leaving nothing out. It was easy for me to create demon fire that could burn with horrific heat. But we needed to be more careful than that. Binding the other demons with our flame without harming them would take both of us and our skills—and it was vital that we harmed no one. Only together could we create enough cold fire to hold the Council members long enough for Cora to give Rathbine the truth potion so we could ask our questions.

When we were finished, Cora excused herself to use the restroom. After she'd gone, Markus gave me a thoughtful look. "She's your mate, isn't she?"

I nodded. "You could tell?"

He shrugged. "The way you looked at her. It was obvious. You're lucky."

A wry laugh escaped me. Lucky? Yes, to have someone like Cora as my mate. But to have a mate at all? It would be easier if I didn't. And yet, I couldn't help but want her.

∽

Cora

. . .

I was grateful to arrive back in New Orleans in one piece. Markus was one of Talan's allies, and his underworld had been one of the better ones as far as I could tell. However, the place had still been terrifying. There had been the strange sense of wrongness there, as if it was a place that wasn't meant for humans like me.

And Markus... There was something dark about him. I couldn't put my finger on whether or not it was evil, but it was something I didn't want to explore.

As soon as we were out of the demon bar and on the quiet, sunny street, I looked up at Talan. "Where are you going to get the potion that will allow me to sneak up on Rathbine? It would have to make me invisible, and block both my scent and my signature. That's not even possible." Last week, Rei had needed to make three potions to achieve that effect, and I hadn't been able to take all three at the same time.

"It's not impossible for Loretta, the leader of the witches. I already sent her a message. She'll hopefully be waiting for us at my place with what we need."

I blew out a low breath. Rei was powerful, but Loretta was another story altogether. "I guess it helps to have friends in high places."

"Oh, she's not a friend. I'm going to owe her."

"It will be worth it."

"Absolutely." The conviction in his voice warmed me. He would do anything to protect his people. I'd been wrong about him from the beginning, but that didn't mean I was wrong to try to stay away from him. Falling for him was just too much.

We headed to Talan's house, which was closest to the demon bar. As expected, Loretta was waiting in one of the sitting rooms near the front door. Her red gown pooled around her small frame and matched the crown of roses atop her head. Dark curls surrounded her face, and her eyes glinted with annoyance as she stood.

"Do you know how long I've been waiting? Five minutes. Five minutes!" She made five minutes sound like five hours, but I had a feeling that nobody made someone like her wait.

"I apologize," Talan said. "And I can't tell you how much we appreciate what you're doing for us. I will owe you a favor."

"You had better."

She stalked toward us and pressed the small potion bottle into his hands. "Be careful with this. It's so powerful that I wasn't willing to trust it to a courier."

"Absolutely." Talan turned to me and handed me the potion. I took it, feeling the faint buzz of magic emanating from the thin glass vial. I slipped it into my pocket.

"It won't last long," she said. "Not more than thirty minutes, so be quick about your business. And good luck." She turned on her heel and stalked from the room. I watched her go, her skirt sweeping the floor as she disappeared around the corner.

I turned to look at Talan. "Can we do this in thirty minutes?"

"We're going to have to."

17

Cora

I walked up to Talan's house like I was going to the gallows. After we'd gotten the potion from Loretta, I'd gone home to check on Fiona. When it was time to return to Talan's house to go to the Council meeting, he had sent a contingent of guards to escort me, as if the trip through town would be deadly.

How strange to have someone care so much about me, someone determined to protect me. In my old life, I'd had no friends and was forced to live the most dangerous life imaginable. So much had changed in a month.

Now I had an abundance of people who cared, and it made me nervous.

What if I lost them? It was almost easier not to have them at all.

I shook the thought away and focused on what was to come. When we went to the meeting of the Demon Council, we wouldn't have guards. It would be risky and dangerous in the extreme. Loretta's potion burned a hole in my pocket, I patted it to make sure it was still there.

The main door to Talan's home opened as I stepped onto the first step. He smiled at me and nodded, then stepped back so I could enter.

"Are you sure you want to come?" he asked. "Liora will happily take your place."

"No." I made my voice hard. "No way in hell am I handing this over. Fiona is counting on me."

He nodded. "You're a good friend."

"Lead the way."

Talan turned and led me through the quiet hall. We saw no one as we headed for the basement. My heart thundered in my chest as we neared the bottom of the steps. Sickly magic emanated from the portal, and it made my skin crawl.

As we approached it, I braced myself for the trip to Talan's underworld. The magic seeping from the portal repulsed me, and the idea of getting into it made my stomach turn.

"It doesn't always feel like this." Talan frowned. "It's been getting worse as the spell strengthens."

"We'll fix it."

"You'll need to take the potion before we go. As soon as we arrive, there will be eyes on us."

"And I only have thirty minutes of invisibility?"

"Approximately. We'll make this quick."

I withdrew the potion from my pocket and uncorked it, my hand shaking slightly. The proximity of the portal and its dark magic was giving me the shivers. I threw back the potion, grimacing at the sour taste. It burned its way to my stomach, and my entire body tingled. "Can you see me?"

"Not a bit. I can't smell you or sense your magic, either."

"Excellent. But how will you know where I am or if I'm in place for the plan to start?" That was a problem, one I hadn't thought of, and it made me nervous. I could be in trouble, and he would have no idea.

"I might not be able to sense you or your magic, but I can feel your proximity through our mate bond. If something goes wrong, and you are in danger, I'll sense it."

It was a relief to hear it, although if something *did* go wrong, we'd be so outnumbered we'd probably be screwed, no matter what. There was no point in saying it, though. "Let's go, then."

He held out his hand. I gripped it and was immediately comforted by his touch. I didn't want to feel this way about him, but I did.

"I've got your back," he said. "I'll always have your back."

His words made my throat tighten, and I felt vaguely silly. But there was something about the way that Talan said it—like he would throw himself in front of a train to protect me. I nodded. "Thank you. Likewise."

Likewise? That was really the best I could do?

Under the circumstances, yeah. I was never great with words, and when I was scared, what little ability I did have went in the toilet.

Talan stepped toward the portal, and I followed, holding my breath as the ether sucked us in. The ride made my stomach pitch. The portal spat us out in the middle of a black and red wasteland.

The meeting was being held at Rathbine's estate. Just our luck.

It had been impossible to change the location, though, and we would have to make do.

It was more horrible than I could have imagined. The air was scented heavily with smoke and blood, the ground pitch black and bisected by scars of bright red. A river of molten silver passed to my right.

Ahead of us, the castle rose toward dark clouds. The jagged black parapets looked like evil incarnate, and the pennants that waved in the wind were the color of blood.

I looked up at Talan. He seemed unusually tense. No wonder if this was where he had been kept prisoner when he was younger. It made me want to tear Rathbine's throat out with my hands. Screw my death magic, I wanted to feel his blood.

"We got this." My voice was soft, but the words seemed to relax Talan.

He nodded and strode forward. I followed, still gripping his hand tightly. It was the best way to let him know where I was. And anyway, I liked it.

At the gate, the guards scrambled to open the massive wooden structure for him. The anxiety in their eyes made me grin. Talan struck fear into the heart of his former captors, and I could imagine nothing more satisfying.

We walked through the gate and across the courtyard, passing a group of skeletal trees that swung with the bodies of dead demons. Bile rose in my throat, and I was suddenly grateful for my life at the orphanage. It had been horrible, and so had my time as an assassin, but it was nothing compared to this place.

Talan truly was from the worst underworld. It made me more determined to help him protect his turf in New Orleans. He could never come back here, nor could his people. We'd find a way to recover the ones who'd disappeared, no matter what it took.

We climbed the steps to the main door, which was held open by uniformed guards. As we entered the dark and dreary foyer, I spotted Markus across the hall. He was dressed in the same simple black clothing, looking like a specter as he hovered near a large door. The fire on a massive hearth cast red shadows across his face, highlighting the scar that cut through his brow.

Markus nodded slightly to Talan, then turned and entered the room. I followed, grasping Talan by the wrist so he could relax the hand I'd been holding. Didn't want anyone to notice his hand in a strange position from clasping mine.

We entered a massive space with a ceiling that was open to the dark gray sky. Black lightning struck through the clouds, and thunder cracked, making my ears ache. The stone walls were draped with tapestries embroidered in shades of black and gray depicting horrific scenes of torture, an odd contrast to the round table in the middle of the room.

Round tables always made me think of Arthur and his honorable knights. The demons who sat around the table were far from honorable. Many of them reeked of black magic, their scent making my stomach turn. Burning tires and rotting bodies and sewage. I breathed shallowly through my mouth, making sure to be silent.

Talan walked to his seat, and I released his hand. He sat across from Markus, and I wondered if that was a strategic move. I slipped away to stand behind Rathbine. He was the worst of the lot—grotesquely hideous, as if the evil in his soul had seeped out to mar his exterior. His scent made my stomach turn, and I did my best to hold my breath. Fear skated over my skin as the demon to Rathbine's left turned to look at me.

Could he somehow sense me?

Please, no.

The demons around the table murmured to each other, waiting for the others to arrive. Anxiety tugged at me. The meeting needed to start. I could already feel the potion starting to wane. Or maybe that was my nerves?

Either way, I wanted to get a move on.

A demon stood, his pale gray frame gaunt and skeletal. The one who had been looking at me turned to face him, and I released the breath I held.

Power wafted from the emaciated demon as he spoke. "We have been called together for an emergency meeting. Council member Talan has something of great importance to share with us." He pinned Talan with his black-eyed stare. "What is it?"

Talan rose to his feet, and the rest of the demons watched in silence. "I have come with an accusation against another Council member."

The skeletal demon frowned. "Of course, you have proof before you speak?"

Dammit. Talan had made it clear how important it was to have proof before one brought an accusation to the Council. In my fantasy world, they'd ignored the requirement and heard him out. I'd secretly hoped they might Interrogate Rathbine, saving me the task ahead.

But nope.

"Not yet, but I will." Talan raised his hands. Green flame erupted from his palms and raced around the room.

Across from him, Markus stood and raised his own hands. Blue fire burst from his palms and shot around the room, twisting around Talan's. The force of the magic made the air rush from my lungs, but fortunately, it didn't come near me.

It twisted around the bodies of the demons sitting at the table, binding them to their chairs. Talan had said there would be no pain, but the demons sure looked pissed.

It was time.

I could feel the last bits of the potion ebbing away. I'd be visible soon. I uncorked the vial and lunged for Rathbine, raising my hand so that I could grip his head with my left and pour the liquid into his mouth with my right.

The demon next to him, who had been so observant, turned to me. His confused expression morphed to surprise, then into a glare. Shock radiated from him, and he burst upward, breaking the fire bonds, and lashed out at me. His arm struck mine, and the truth potion flew from my hand and crashed against the stone floor.

I cried out in surprise and pain. Across the room, Talan jerked at the sound. Fear crossed his face as he searched the room for me.

It was enough to break his focus and cause his flame to flicker. Markus' magic wasn't enough to hold the demons to their seats, and they broke free of their bonds and lunged upright.

Shit.

I darted backward, feeling my body become entirely visible. In front of me, a fight broke out. Every member on the Council turned on another—but surprisingly, they didn't all attack Markus and Talan. They had more allies than they realized.

The demons clashed, blasts of flame exploding around me. I pulled two of Rei's potion bombs from the ether. The demon who had sensed me lumbered toward me. He was huge and fast, a massive sword dangling from one of his large, clawed hands. His demeanor was relaxed as he approached me, but his gaze burned with bloodlust.

I hurled the potion bombs at him, but he dodged them. They exploded against the floor, useless. Shit. I drew two more, but he dodged those too, moving with a swiftness that shocked me.

I drew my karambit from the ether. I couldn't use my death magic against anyone here—the questions afterward would be too deadly.

But could I defend myself with just a knife?

I'd have to.

"What exactly were you attempting to do, little

bird?" The endearment rumbled out of the demon's chest, almost chiding.

Anger rose inside me. He'd ruined my plan, and he'd called me *little freaking bird*.

Hell no.

My fury gave me extra speed. I lunged for him, putting all my strength into it. Surprise flashed on his face as he raised his blade. I ducked under the sword and sliced into his side with my karambit, then spun to stab him in the shoulder. The steel sunk easily through flesh.

He roared, spinning to face me. Rage twisted his face as blood dripped down his side. "You'll pay for that."

His large sword sliced through the air, so fast that it took all my skill to dodge the blade. I felt the air woosh over my head as I ducked, and fear chilled my skin.

I'd gotten lucky before. He was too fast for me to fight with a blade, so I'd need to be clever.

Out of the corner of my eye, I could see two demons throwing fire at each other in massive blasts. I darted toward them, drawing my attacker with me. I gripped the karambit in a throwing hold, then threw it at one of the demons.

The blade sank into his thigh, and he roared in pain, spinning to face us. Flame flickered around his palm as he raised it and hurled another blast. I ducked, and it slammed into the demon behind me. He screamed and dropped to the ground, rolling as he tried to douse the flames.

I spun back to the demon who had thrown the fire. He was already fending off the attack of another.

Whew.

I'd gotten lucky there.

"Stop!" Talan's roar rose over the sound of battle. His flame burst to life around us, green fire flickering toward the ceiling.

His tone was so commanding that the demons actually listened. The green fire probably also had something to do with it. It was hot enough to burn us all alive. They turned to face him.

CHAPTER 18

Talan

The Council members turned to stare at me, glaring daggers.

Not ideal.

On the far side of the room, I spotted Rathbine's body.

That was worse.

"What's the meaning of this?" Belial demanded. Rathbine's female poker partner glared at me, fire erupting from her red hair.

This was not how I'd hoped this would go. It would be nearly impossible to convince them to hear me out, especially since Rathbine was unconscious. Or dead.

It would be too much to hope for the latter.

My gaze moved briefly to Cora, who looked mostly

unharmed. Relief rushed through me. It had been fear for her that had broken my control earlier. Now that painlessly binding the Council members was no longer an option, I'd have to use the full extent of my demon flame. It would just piss them off, but at least they would be forced to listen.

"Rathbine has been encroaching on my territory," I said. "Part of his plan involved manipulating my portal to Evonec, which has resulted in my people disappearing."

"Disappearing?" Falco asked. The slender demon was almost an ally, and I appreciated the question.

Everyone seemed to be listening, so I let my ring of fire die—for now. "Kidnapped. Killed. We don't know yet."

"And this entire thing"—he gestured around him—"was meant to get your proof?"

I nodded, looking toward Rathbine's body. "Because the Council forbids accusations without proof, and we're running out of time, we planned to dose Rathbine with a truth potion and force him to admit what he's done in front of the Council."

Falco nodded, his brows rising. He looked impressed, thank fates. He just as easily could have been enraged, but demons respected cunning. If I was proven right about Rathbine, they would forgive my transgression.

"Bad news, though," Markus said from across the

room where he knelt over the body of Rathbine. "He's unconscious and can't be revived."

"He can't confess to anything, then," Valberith said, a grin cutting through his ephemeral features. "And you should be punished for your transgressions."

That confirmed it. Valberith was definitely on the side of Rathbine.

"I want the truth," Falco said. "It was a huge risk to stage and attack at a meeting of the Council. If Talan did so, he truly believes that Rathbine is responsible for interfering with his realm. And if that's the case, Rathbine has broken the greatest law of them all. We need to know."

There were murmurs of agreement, thank fates. If I'd been accusing Rathbine of anything else, they probably wouldn't have listened. No one wanted another demon meddling in their realm, and if Rathbine would do it to me, he could do it to others.

"It's inappropriate," Belial said. "He's accused without proof."

"We know that," Falco hissed in annoyance. "But I want to hear him out. These are extenuating circumstances."

"But we can't ask Rathbine until he wakes," Valberith said. "*If* he wakes."

"I'll take a truth potion," I said. "One that has been provided by one of you so that you know it's effective."

"We would never allow that as evidence!" Valberith shouted.

He was right. It had never been done before, or I might have tried it instead of this crazy plan.

"At the very least, it will show that he believes what he's saying," Falco said.

"If this were any other crime, I wouldn't stand for it," Markus said. "I wouldn't have helped him. But we can't have a Council member attacking the realm of another. We need to know."

There was more grumbling, but enough demons seemed in favor of my plan that one was sent to retrieve a truth potion. Tension laced the air as we waited, and I kept my gaze trained on Cora.

So far, everyone had been so offended by my actions —or afraid of my fire—that they hadn't mentioned her. She'd crept to a corner and was hiding in the shadows, and I hoped it would stay that way.

A moment later, a servant returned to the room with a small glass vial. They brought it to me, and I uncorked it. I sniffed, catching the telltale scent of hellbane that was found in truth potions. Satisfied, I tossed it back.

"Repeat your accusation," Falco said.

I did, the words flowing easily from my tongue. I believed it because it was true. The potion didn't stop me from speaking, and I could see the expressions change on the other demon's faces. Some became angry, others looked worried. The worried ones could be his allies. I'd have to remember them.

When I was done speaking, Falco turned to the others. He'd taken on the role of moderator, and I was glad no one objected.

"Well?" he asked. "I believe him. Do you?"

"You have to," Markus said. "He took the truth potion. His words cannot be a lie."

"But he could still be wrong even if he believes his words are true," Valberith said, his wispy form hovering over the ground.

"Has anyone ever known Talan to make mistakes?" Markus asked. "He's right about this, and I believe him."

"We'll put Rathbine in a cell until he revives. When he does, we'll give him a truth potion," Valberith said.

"No." My voice boomed through the room. "I need him to break the spell he's placed on the portal. I'll be taking him with me."

Valberith glared. "We can't let you do that."

"You'll have no choice. I'm taking him."

"And I suppose you're taking the woman, too?" Valberith turned and pointed to Cora, who was still tucked into the shadows. "Don't think we forgot about her and the role she played. Outsiders aren't invited to our meetings."

Anger roared to life inside me, dark and powerful. Flames erupted around me, a testament to my rage.

When I spoke, it vibrated in my voice. "Touch her, and I will destroy you."

An uneasy silence descended. I might not survive my attempt at destruction, but I would take many of them with me. I was the most powerful demon there, and they were aware. My wrath would cut down at least half the Council, if not more.

No one was willing to find out which half they'd be on.

"Fine," Valberith said. "Take Rathbine. But if he doesn't wake and give you proof within twenty-four hours, we're coming for you."

I nodded curtly. Markus had already thrown his lot in with us, so he scooped Rathbine up and flung him over his shoulder, then strode to the door. I walked to Cora and stayed close by her side as we left.

Cora

I stumbled through the portal, gasping as I arrived back in Talan's house. The last hour had been horrific. Not only the battle, but also our departure, my back burning from the angry gazes of the demons. I'd expected one of them to throw a knife at me as we left.

Markus escorted us to the portal near Rathbine's home and handed the unconscious body over to Talan.

We bound him in the magic cuffs that I'd taken off my attacker earlier this week. Swinging Rathbine over his shoulder like a sack of potatoes, the demon lord had gripped my hand and stepped through the portal.

I looked at him now, standing tall and powerful with the unconscious demon over his shoulder. Worry creased his brow as he asked, "Are you all right?"

"Yeah, just a little shaky." I dragged a hand through my hair. "I knew it was going to get dicey, but I didn't expect an outright battle."

"We got lucky." He turned toward the door, where Liora had just appeared. "Can you get two guards to take Rathbine to the healer? See if she can revive him."

Liora nodded and turned, shouting down the hall. A few moments later, two guards appeared. They took Rathbine's body and carried him away.

Liora arched an eyebrow. "I take it that it didn't go the way you hoped?"

"Not quite. But if we can revive him and get him to admit the truth, then we know he's the one who can remove the spell from the portal."

"Any idea how you might get him to do that?"

"He's a coward. It won't be a problem." Talan turned to me. "Let me see you back to your house."

"I'll be fine."

"The fae queen is still angry with us, and she could have sent her guards into the city to capture us. It'd be safer if I escorted you back."

I couldn't argue with that. "Thanks. I want to check on Fiona, then I'll come back to see how Rathbine is doing."

I couldn't believe we might be close to our solution. All we needed was confirmation from Rathbine that he could remove the spell on the portal, then we'd force him to do it. I had faith that Talan could scare him into anything he wanted.

And if he couldn't, I would.

Talan escorted me to the city, staying close as we walked. I could feel his worried gaze on me, but I said nothing. We'd made it out alive with most of our goals accomplished, so that was all that mattered. By the time I got back to my house, I was desperate to make sure Fiona was okay, and to take a shower. My hair smelled like Rathbine's realm, and it made my stomach turn.

Talan opened the bookstore door for me. "I'll walk you upstairs."

I stepped through. "I'm good from here."

"I don't mind. It will make me feel better." Talan followed me up the stairs to our living room.

Relief rushed through me when I saw Fiona sitting on the couch next to Balthazar. The black shadow cat was still curled up on his toaster on the side table. He ignored us, but Fiona leapt to her feet, a grin on her face. "You're back! Did you get Rathbine?"

"Yes, but he's—"

Fiona cried out, her face twisted in panic. Her form

began to flicker in and out of existence. I lunged for her, wrapping my arms around her waist.

"It's so strong," she gasped, clutching me tightly.

Whatever was pulling at her was stronger than it had ever been. Because we were bound together by Rei's magical bracelet, I could feel a tug on my own soul. I was also losing my grip on her no matter how hard I held on.

"No! Fiona!" I cried.

It wasn't enough. With one last shout, she disappeared. I felt her loss like an amputated limb, and something strange pulled at me—as if the portal was trying to drag me along, too. If it got any stronger, it might succeed.

I spun to face Talan, panic thudding in my head and drowning out rational thought. "We have to get to Rathbine and make him remove the spell."

"I'm not sure that will work," Talan's voice was soft with worry. He walked to me, gripping my arms gently in what he probably thought was a comforting touch. But nothing could comfort me right now.

"Why?"

"If she's already gone, it won't matter if the portal is repaired."

"But where did she go? We have to go get her."

Talan frowned, his face creasing in confusion as he inhaled through his nose. "What's that smell? It's sulfur, but something else."

"I don't know. I've never smelled anything like it." Strange scents filled the air, something vile but unidentifiable.

He sniffed the air again, his frown deepening. "I think I know it. The Falls of Malach in my realm. It's halfway between my land and Rathbine's."

Hope flared to life inside me, terrifying in its strength. "You think the portal brought her there?"

"I think it's our best bet. It's obviously taking them somewhere, and we spoke to that family earlier in the week. The daughter said she smelled sulfur when her mother was taken."

"But she might not have caught the other scent," I said, understanding dawning. "But you recognize it because you've been there."

"We need to go there. Now." There was hope in his eyes, and it made mine flare brighter.

"Let's go." I looked back at Balthazar, who was shooting a worried glance between me and the space where Fiona had just stood. "Don't worry, buddy. I'll get her back."

I believed it. I had to. I couldn't bear the thought of losing her. Failing her. The pain of it was so unexpected, worse than anything I'd ever felt. I'd never lost someone before, not someone I truly cared about.

We ran from the house, pushing our way through the crowd on the street as we sprinted toward Talan's home. I pulled my phone from my pocket and shot a quick message to Rei and Mia. They would want to come, and we could use backup. I tugged on Talan's arm. "Why don't you call Calex and see if he'll help."

He pulled out his phone, quickly calling Calex. When we arrived at Talan's house, we went immediately to the cell where Rathbine was being held. If he was conscious, he would be able to confirm our suspicions.

Unfortunately, he was still out cold. The healer bent over him, frowning. She looked up at us. "He's still alive and in relatively good shape, considering. But I'm not sure when he'll revive."

"Could he travel?" Talan asked.

"If someone carries him, I don't see why not."

Talan looked at the guards. "Are you willing to come on a mission to Evonec? We're going to retrieve the demons who were taken from our realm. But I don't want this one out of my sight, especially if he revives. I'll need help carrying him."

Both men nodded eagerly, gripping their sword hilts tight. The one on the left threw Rathbine over his shoulder and said, "Let's go, boss."

Talan turned for the door, and the four of us strode back toward the portal in the basement. Calex was already waiting there with Mia and Rei at his side. Together, we descended the stairs. Liora waited by the portal, ready to go.

"You know where they are?" she asked.

"The Falls of Malach." Talan nodded toward Rathbine's unconscious body. "As soon as Rathbine revives, we'll make him remove the spell on the portal. We can't lose any more people if we are wrong about the location."

Excitement rose in my chest, along with hope and fear. It was a strange, volatile mixture.

I looked at Mia and Rei. "Are you guys ready?"

"Absolutely." Rei raised her bag full of potions. "Just in case you need a few."

"Definitely. Thank you."

Talan reached for my hand, and I gripped his without thinking. But the fear I felt over losing Fiona echoed in my mind. What I was beginning to feel for Talan was just as strong. Stronger, actually. I couldn't bear to watch him die. I pulled my hand from his. The portal was set to take us to a specific place, so we didn't technically need to be holding hands to end up at the same destination.

He shot me a questioning glance.

"Let's just go," I said.

He nodded curtly. "The portal will take us to my home. From there, we'll have to take carriages to the Falls of Malach in the Dark Forest."

"Lead the way," Calex said.

One by one, we stepped through the portal. I let the either suck me in, spinning me through space, and wished that I'd held onto Talen's hand.

I was a mess. Why did no one tell me that emotions were hard?

The portal spat us out in the middle of a darkened wasteland. It was even worse than the place where Rathbine lived, the red and black sky lit with fierce white lightning. Fiery red mountains rose tall in the distance, and plains of black wheat waved in the breeze.

Talan raised his fingers to his mouth and gave a piercing whistle. From the estate in the distance, three teams of horses galloped toward us. Each group of four pulled racing carriages and approached us at lightning speed.

As the horses neared, I realized they were far from normal. They were made of bone and black fire, their eyes gleaming red—just like the ones that had galloped past Markus's estate. The carriages were built of steel and wood, with shields decorating their sides. They reminded me of a picture I'd seen of Viking long ships that carried warriors to battle. The horses stopped abruptly, stamping their hooves and breathing fire.

"They know where to go. Just climb on." Talan got onto the nearest carriage, then leaned down to offer me a hand. I took it, because I didn't want to be a total weirdo, and let him haul me up into the carriage. Calex climbed onto the bench next to me. Rei, Mia, and Liora took the other carriage. The two demon guards carried Rathbine's limp body into the third.

As soon as we were seated, the demon horses took

off. They accelerated into a gallop, moving so swiftly that I was forced to grip the wooden seat beneath me for support. The carriage sped over the hardened ground, the horses sending up clouds of dark dust. They breathed so hard that fire shot from their nostrils.

Overhead, lightning struck, the accompanying thunder rattling my lungs in my chest. On the horizon, a dark forest lurked. It grew larger as we approached, and the leafless branches looked like skeletal hands reaching toward the lightning-streaked sky.

A shiver ran down my spine.

"That's the forest. The Falls of Malach should be just inside." Talan stared at it, his face grim. "I never visit. It's a terrible place."

"I hope the kidnapped demons are unconscious. I would hate for them to remember this." Just the idea of Fiona trapped in there made ice chill my skin.

The horses pulled to a stop in front of a tree line. There was no way the carriages could enter—the trees were too close together, their roots protruding from the ground.

Talan climbed down from the carriage. "We will have to go on foot."

I followed him down, watching as he pulled a shield from the side of the carriage. I did the same, holding it in front of my chest. I didn't know what we would face in there, but I would be following Talan's lead in everything. He had the most experience, and

I'd been in this game too long to ignore that kind of thing.

The others took their own shields, and we approached the forest on silent feet. The guards who carried Rathbine lingered toward the back, and Talan turned to them. "Keep up if you can. But if it's too dangerous, get out of here. I despise Rathbine, but I don't want an unconscious man to be killed because of me."

The two guards nodded, and we continued into the forest. I stuck close by my friends, searching the forest around us for threats. Every time lightning struck, the trees cast skeletal shadows on the ground. It was a strange, terrible sight. Especially once darkness began to roll over my boots. It reeked like the portal's magic.

This was definitely the place.

We hadn't gone far when I heard the sound of rustling in the distance. I searched the darkness around me, taking advantage of every blast of lightning to see better. When I caught sight of figures through the trees, I gasped. "Talan, there are guards up ahead on the left."

"They're wearing Rathbine's colors." Grim satisfaction colored his voice.

"There are fae guards, too," Calex pointed to the right. "They wear the queen's colors."

I squinted at them, spotting the telltale sign of bows and arrows. "They're armed with bows," I said. "Duck!"

Arrows flew out of the forest, fired with terrifying

skill. They sparkled with magic. I raised my shield and ducked behind it. Arrows pinged off the front, one after the other. All around me, my friends crouched near the ground, arrows hitting their shields.

"The damned arrows are enchanted not to miss," Rei said.

Next to me, Talan pressed his hands to the ground. Flame raced from his palms, streaking between the tree roots as it shot toward the attacking fae.

I peered around my shield, watching as the flame surrounded them in a circle. The fae screamed, turning and running from the inferno. In his own realm, the demon lord was impossibly strong. The fire reached toward the sky, ascending past the tips of the trees.

I looked at Talan. "Won't that start a forest fire? If Fiona and the others are unconscious, they could be trapped in it."

"No, the trees are strengthened by demon fire." He pointed. The trees weren't catching fire. They were growing even taller.

Wow.

"Let's move," Talan stood, his demon fire still flickering amongst the trees.

We followed him through the woods, looking for Rathbine's guards who had disappeared when Talan's inferno erupted.

The scent that had drawn us there grew stronger. I almost thought I could hear the sound of the waterfall when the first blast of red fire struck the ground near my feet.

I lunged to the side, looking up to see Rathbine's guards hiding high amongst the tree branches. They had climbed up onto the limbs.

Rei tossed me some of her potion bombs, and I hurled them up toward the demons in the trees, hitting one with an explosive blast. His body plummeted, crashing on the twisted roots below.

Rei threw another bomb at a demon above her. The bomb connected, and the demon fell. She dodged out of the way, narrowly avoiding being crushed. Calex and Talan aimed blasts of fire at the hearts of the demons, taking three of them out of the trees. I watched with satisfaction as they plummeted to the ground.

The rest continued to throw fireballs, hurling brilliant blasts of red fire. I raised my shield and ducked, but there were too many demons. Fire was coming from all directions. A blast hit me in the shoulder, so hot and fierce that I cried out. Talan was at my side in an instant, positioning his shield to cover my back.

Mia raised her hands, directing her magic toward the trees. The tree branches shook, and the remaining demons tumbled from the limbs. I looked over at Mia, impressed. Her face was pale and wan, her shoulders slumped. She looked like hell. The maneuver must have used up all her magic, and she'd need time to recover.

I caught Calex's eye. "Stay close to Mia."

He nodded and moved to her.

I looked around at the rest of my friends, many of whom were worse for wear. We'd survived the fae and Rathbine's demons, but our enemy had left their mark. People's clothes were singed in places, revealing burned flesh. But everyone was on their feet, and that was victory enough. Even Talan's guards had managed to keep up, protecting Rathbine's unconscious body.

That bastard had better wake up soon.

CHAPTER 19

Talan

With all of Rathbine's demons dead and the fae having run off, it was safe enough to leave our position and head toward the sound of water. As we neared the waterfall, something tightened in my chest.

Was it hope or fear? Probably both.

I would never forget the faces of the family members as they told me about their missing loved ones. I prayed to the gods that I didn't believe in that we would find them.

Next to me, Cora moved silently. She was an excellent fighter, the best I had ever seen. It helped keep her safe, but I felt a jolt of fear every time someone attacked her.

I caught sight of the falls, the blood red water

pouring down the black rocks. To the left of the falls, a glowing red cage contained the bodies of the missing demons. They lay quiet and still.

Cora cried out and ran toward the cage.

"Be careful!" I called, racing after her.

She stopped just short of the bars to search the faces of the fallen. I spotted Fiona almost immediately, lying in the middle of the group. She appeared to be unconscious, her eyes closed and her form still.

Cora whirled to face me. "How do we get them out?"

I hovered my hand over the bars. Violent magic sparked within them. There was a strange blue glow surrounding the red, something I had never seen before. "I don't know. We likely need the person who cast the spell."

"Rathbine or the fae queen."

The others joined us, staring into the cage.

"I feel their magic," Rei whispered. "Like it's flowing out of them."

She was right. Their magic hung heavy on the air.

But there was more magic coming from behind us. It was intensely powerful and distinctly fae. I turned, spotting the fae queen. She drifted between the skeletal trees, wearing a suit of glittering armor with a sword dangling from her hand. Her golden hair had been piled on her head around a crown of deadly spikes. Weapons as her jewels.

Behind her, a horde of fae followed dressed in battle armor, their faces twisted with menace.

The queen's brows rose, and she gave us a cold smile. "I heard there was a disturbance."

"Why have you done this?" I demanded.

"For the power, of course." She raised her hand, magic glowing from her palm. "There's just so much of it waiting to be taken from their souls!" Her grin was manic.

She glowed with the same pale blue light that filled the cage, and suddenly, it all made sense. She and Rathbine had joined forces. In exchange for her magic, she got the power of the fallen demons. He had done the grunt work, and when my realm was devoid of my demons, he would take our land. He'd always wanted it, and with the fae queen's help, he'd found a way to get it.

Over my dead body.

"It's far more than a disturbance." I stepped forward, my hands flickering with green flame, and hurled the blast at her. She lashed out, deflecting the flame with her sword.

Shock lanced me. She'd grown far more powerful from the magic she'd taken. She thrust her hand forward and screamed, "Attack!"

Her army charged, their boots pounding the ground. There were too many of them. We had the skill, but not enough power.

I looked back at the glowing cage, then gripped one

of the bars, feeling the power surge into me. I combined it with my own magic and sent a massive blast of green flame at the encroaching fae. It slammed into a dozen of them, throwing them backward.

Next to me, Rei did the same. She gripped the bar, then threw out her hand. The earth split in front of the queen, halting her forward progress. She glared, reaching down to touch the ground. It began to knit itself back together.

"If we can kill the queen, the others might stop," Cora said.

A wave of fae was nearly to us, their swords raised. I sent another blast of flame, taking them out, but more came.

Mia grabbed the cage, letting the power infuse her as she manipulated the tree limbs into wrapping around a group of fae and yanking them upward. She took out nearly a dozen, yet there were still more. So many more. The queen seemed to be conjuring them from nowhere, and I wasn't sure they were even alive. They could just be figments of her magic, but deadly all the same.

Unfortunately, she seemed to have an endless well of magic.

Next to me, Cora gripped my arm. "She's too strong. I'm going to have to get closer."

"She'll kill you."

"Then provide cover, so I can sneak up."

"Absolutely not." That same fear tugged at my soul

again. I couldn't let her approach alone, putting herself at risk.

"You know it's the only way. She can deflect any magic that she sees coming, but she doesn't know what I have."

I hated it, but Cora was right. The queen didn't know what Cora could do with just a touch. Every inch of my soul objected, but I nodded tightly. Mate bond or no, I had to trust that Cora could do what she said.

As much as I wanted to wrap her in protection, I couldn't stop her. She was powerful—massively so—and she made her own choices.

"Go." It hurt like hell to say the word, but I forced it out.

She nodded and slipped off through the woods. I caught the attention of the others and said, "Create a distraction for Cora. Throw everything you have at the queen."

My companions nodded, launching volleys of magic at the oncoming fae. Rei split the earth, and Mia shook the trees. Calex and I threw fire, massive blasts exploding in the forest.

But it wouldn't be enough.

From behind the queen and her line of fae, I caught sight of Cora creeping out from between the trees. Her gaze was glued to the queen. As if the queen could sense her, she whirled around.

I called upon my magic, hurling a massive blast of

flame at her. It hit her in the back, but she stayed standing. Fear iced my skin as she reached out a hand and used her magic to draw Cora to her. I watched in horror as my mate was yanked across the ground and into the queen's grasp. The fae wrapped her hand around Cora's throat, squeezing tight.

I roared and charged, but the fae army closed in between me and my target.

"You thought you could sneak up on me?" The queen cackled. "And what? Attack me with your little blade?"

Desperately, I fought my way through the hordes of fae, throwing fireballs and breaking necks. Blades sliced at me, some plunging deep, but I kept going, driven by a desperate need to get to Cora. To protect her.

"No." Cora raised a hand and touched the queen's cheek. The queen stiffened and dropped to the ground. She released her grip on Cora, and my mate stumbled.

All around me, fae began to disappear, most of them created by the queen. The few that were left standing took off at a run, sprinting into the forest. I didn't bother to go after them or command the others to hunt them. They were no longer a threat.

Aching, I strode toward Cora. She gasped, rubbing her neck.

"That was close." She shivered. "I hate to use that magic." Her gaze moved to the waterfall behind me, then to the cage. Hope lit her eyes, and a huge smile spread across her face. "The cage is gone. It disappeared when the queen died. Just like her army."

She raced around me, limping as she ran toward the unmoving bodies. She had suffered a horrific burn on her side, but it didn't slow her down. As she reached them, they began to sit up. Many moved slowly, groaning as they rubbed their heads.

Before Cora could reach Fiona, a blast of flame shot from behind me, flying over my shoulder to slam into her back. She fell forward, a scream escaping her lips. I whirled, hurling a massive blast of demon fire at whoever had attacked her. Just before the giant blast made contact, I spotted Rathbine. At his side lay the guard who'd held the keys to Rathbine's magic cuffs. The bastard must've regained consciousness and taken him by surprise. My blast of fire slammed into Rathbine, throwing him backward. The flame roared, incinerating him.

Within seconds, he lay dead.

I raced to Cora's side and fell to my knees. Her back was scorched, and a spike of fear drove into my heart.

"Healer!" I roared. "I need a healer!"

Cora's chest was moving slowly with every breath. She was still alive, but for how long? Pain like I'd never known twisted through me.

"I'm a healer, I'm a healer!" A demon stumbled toward me, having just awoken from the spell that had bound him. His magic smelled of green grass and oranges. He knelt beside Cora, resting his hands gently against her shoulders. His magic flared on the air as he fed it into her. A grin spread across his face. "I still have my power."

"All of it?" I hoped so, for Cora's sake.

"I think so. I felt it return to me when the queen died. We could feel her sucking our magic out. We could feel *everything*."

Everything? That was barbaric. Anger lit up within me. I was glad she was dead.

Before my eyes, Cora's skin healed. Mia, Rei, and Fiona joined us, staring worriedly at Cora. Though there were more injuries in our group, Cora had taken the worst of it.

When she groaned, relief rushed through me. The skin of her back looked unblemished, and she rolled over. Her gaze went immediately to Fiona, and she cried out and reached up to hug her friend.

I sat back on my heels, grateful to see her whole and healthy.

Cora

Joy lit within me as I hugged Fiona. It was only once I pulled back that I realized something was different about her.

She was no longer partially transparent.

I blinked at her. "What happened to you?"

"What do you mean?" Fiona frowned at herself, then gasped. She held up her hands and inspected them. They looked like normal hands, totally opaque and flesh colored. Her gaze met mine, excitement rushing into her face. "Do I have a heartbeat?"

I pressed my head to her chest and heard a heartbeat. I pulled back, shocked. "You do!"

"I don't understand." She looked around, her gaze landing on Mia and Rei. "What happened?"

"No idea," Rei said.

I looked at the other demons. They'd struggled to their feet and were crying and hugging each other. It was the happiest thing I've ever seen, but still... What had happened to Fiona?

An older woman pushed through the crowd toward us. She reached out to touch Fiona's cheek, and a smile lit her face.

"You know what happened to me?" Fiona asked.

"I think I might." The woman's gaze moved over Fiona's body. "I was the first to be taken. Every time another joined us, I could feel our life forces merge, along with our magic. You were the last, so you didn't feel it. But I think it's possible that each person in that cage shared a little bit of their life force with you. It was part of the spell that leached our magic away. A happy side effect."

Fiona's jaw slackened her brows rose. "I can't believe it. But are you okay?"

"Fine, dear." She smiled. "There are more than enough of us to share a little bit with you and the other ghost who was captured with us."

Fiona laughed joyfully. "I can't believe it. I'm alive." She looked at me and hugged me hard, then gasped and pulled back. "Oh, my God. I remember how I died!"

"Really?" I could feel Talan watching me, but I didn't care. I wanted to know how my friend was, and I was reveling in the fact that she was okay.

"I discovered that your mother was stealing books from orphans, so I confronted her. She blasted me with magic. I'm not sure if she meant to kill me, but I got unlucky, and a bookshelf fell on me."

"A bookshelf fell on you?" A surprised laugh escaped me. "I'm so glad that you came back to life, because that is a seriously ridiculous way to die."

"I know. The shame of it." Fiona laughed and buried her face in her hands. "No wonder the dead have a hard time remembering how they died. It's pretty horrific."

"I'm glad you know." I smiled. "Figuring it out was my job, though. I'll have to find another way to make it up to you, considering that it was my mother who killed you."

"You owe me nothing." Fiona gave me a playful punch to the shoulder. "Anyway, you saved me, and that definitely counts."

I threw my arms around her, then felt Mia and Rei join the huddle. We hugged each other and laughed, grateful to be alive.

Eventually, we pulled apart and stood. Talan had gone to check on the other demons, and the healer was tending to the worst of the wounds. Our surroundings were terrible, but the relief and joy we felt made it not quite as bad.

All the same, I was glad when we left the forest as a massive group. Talan gave a piercing whistle, then caught my gaze and said, "We'll need more carriages. The horses can hear me, even from a distance."

By the time we made it out of the forest, there were more carriages waiting for us.

I shared one with Mia, Rei, and Fiona, who chatted the entire time about what she was going to eat and how she was going to change her clothes. I couldn't help but grin, the joy nearly overwhelming. Every now and again, I looked toward Talan, unable to help myself.

As soon as we stepped through the portal to New Orleans, I could tell that it was back to normal. It looked —and smelled—completely benign. The others had gone first, and many had already left the room, hurrying up the stairs to be reunited with their families. Fiona, Mia, and Rei stood near the door, waiting for me.

"Are you coming?" Fiona asked.

"Yes. Give me a moment. I'll meet you outside."

She nodded, and they left.

I turned to Talan, who was the only one left in the room. I nodded toward the portal. "How did it get fixed?"

"You didn't see it, but Rathbine woke and attacked you. I killed him." He dragged a hand through his hair. "I'm just grateful that the spell on the portal died with him."

I blew out a shuddering breath. No kidding. Many spells died with the death of their caster, but not all. Talan's instinct to kill anyone who attacked me might have cost us the ability to break the spell on the portal.

He had put his entire realm at risk for me.

His gaze met mine, and I could tell that he was thinking the same thing. There was a serious expression in his eyes and tension around his mouth.

"I don't know what to do," he said. "I care for you. I can't help it. You're my mate, but even if you weren't, I would still care for you. And yet, I risked the fate of my realm to protect you."

I could hear torment in his voice. The two possible goals that he held dear--to protect me and protect his realm. When they were pushed up against each other, I had won out. And I didn't think he liked that. It was clear he felt guilty. Clear that he might even regret the action.

Or maybe I was projecting.

Either way, I knew that I couldn't face caring for somebody as much as I cared for Fiona. Nearly losing her had almost broken me, and I couldn't survive something like that again.

If I fell for Talan, I would care for him far more. His loss would cripple me. It had taken everything I had to open myself up enough to make friends. I didn't have it in me to risk anything more—especially considering the fact that my old boss was still after me. I'd evaded him so far, but he wouldn't stop until he got me back. He'd kill anyone in his path to get to me, and I couldn't risk Talan like that.

"It's okay." I drew a deep breath and turned to leave. "I'm going to go. Alone. And I don't want to see you again."

"Wait." Talan gripped my arm gently.

I shook his hand off but didn't turn to face him. "It's better this way. Better for both of us."

"I don't know if I can stay away from you."

"You're going to have to."

And with those words, I left.

THANK YOU FOR READING!

I hope you enjoyed reading this book as much as I enjoyed writing it. Reviews are *so* helpful to authors. I really appreciate all reviews, both positive and negative. If you want to leave one, you can do so at Amazon or GoodReads.

ACKNOWLEDGMENTS

Thank you, Ben, for everything. There would be no books without you.

Thank you to Jena O'Connor and Lexi George for your excellent editing. Thank you Rachel for your eagle eye with spotting errors. The book is immensely better because of you! And thank you Orina Kafe for the beautiful cover.

ABOUT LINSEY

Before becoming a writer, Linsey Hall was a nautical archaeologist who studied shipwrecks from Hawaii and the Yukon to the UK and the Mediterranean. She credits fantasy and historical romances with her love of history and her career as an archaeologist. After a decade of tromping around the globe in search of old bits of stuff that people left lying about, she settled down and started penning her own romance novels. Her Dragon's Gift series draws upon her love of history and the paranormal elements that she can't help but include.

This is a work of fiction. All reference to events, persons, and locale are used fictitiously, except where documented in historical record. Names, characters, and places are products of the author's imagination, and any resemblance to actual events, locales, or persons, living or dead, is coincidental.

Copyright 2022 by Bonnie Doon Press Inc.

Linsey@LinseyHall.com
www.LinseyHall.com
https://twitter.com/HiLinseyHall
https://www.facebook.com/LinseyHallAuthor

Made in United States
Troutdale, OR
06/03/2024

20310061R10159